I0740013

Haste Ye Back

Marilyn Ludwig

ZAFA PUBLISHING
DOWNERS GROVE, IL

In memory of Mary Thale,
who gave me the gift of London

For Mimi and Sandy—part of the adventure

And for N

UNITED KINGDOM

Chapter One

"WHAT ARE YOU HAVING?" DENNIS didn't answer but continued to scribble in his notebook. He hadn't said anything since we'd been introduced back at O'Hare Airport in Chicago. "Guess it's going to be a quiet flight," I muttered.

Across the aisle, Shirl, that's my mother, and her friend, Liza, chose seared fillet of salmon. I settled for a veggie platter for gourmet palates. Dennis's choice was a mystery, for he just opened the menu and pointed when the flight attendant took his order. I was beginning to have doubts, big doubts, about this trip.

The whole thing started last December when I was sitting in the dental hygienist's chair while Shirl caught up with the latest self-help magazines. "Look, Carly," she said, pointing out an article. I glanced at the title. "Today's Youth in Crisis." I shrugged.

"No, look who wrote it. *The prominent child psychologist, Dr. Fiona Douglas.* That was my friend in college—one of my roommates. You know, I always talk about her."

"You mean, Fiffy? The Scottish girl who lived in Peru?" Or was it the other way around? It had never made much sense to me. "Are you sure it's her? Fiona Douglas is probably a common name in Scotland."

Shirl beamed. "Yes, there's a short bio. I always wondered what became of her. Just think—a prominent child psychologist. And it says she'll be giving a lecture in London this summer. I wonder . . ."

That night, Shirl called her other college roommate, Liza Ames, and the plans began. Both of them wrote to Fiona in care of the magazine, and waited. Several months later, Shirl received a reply, a formal printed invitation stating that Dr. Douglas would be honored to have Mrs. Giles Sullivan attend the lecture.

Not very friendly, I thought.

This time, Liza called Shirl. Liza had received an identical invitation and had consulted her husband who said fine, as long as she took along Dennis, their eighteen-year-old son.

Shirl and I only had each other to consult. We both said fine.

Now, I wasn't so sure about the "fine" part. Liza and Shirl could share "Do you remembers" all the way to England, but Dennis had turned out to be plain awful. Not only was he glum and silent, he wasn't much to look at—shaggy black hair, a wrinkled Grateful Dead tee shirt, an earring and, even worse, he reeked of stale cigarette smoke. I hoped he had been listening when the flight attendant warned about tampering with the smoke detector in the lav.

Our dinners arrived, served on cream-colored china set on pale blue linen. Liza's husband, a frequent flyer, had upgraded our tickets to Business Class. Truly elegant.

Dennis had chosen veal with thyme. Veal! Another strike against him.

"Carly, would you like to try a bite of my salmon?"

"No, but thanks, Shirl," I replied.

Dennis put down his fork. "Why do you call your mother Shirl?"

Whatayaknow? It speaks! I tried to be friendly. "I'm not sure. I always have. My father died when I was little. Shirl and I are more like friends than anything else."

"Whatever."

So much for that.

Liza glanced over and frowned, and then went back to chatting with Shirl, who looked happier and more relaxed than I'd seen her in ages.

Shirl's had it rough. Not only does she have a mild heart condition, she's got a chronic worrying condition—about money, politics, global warming, me . . . You name it, Shirl's worried about it. She teaches second grade during the year and usually gets temp work in the summer. Her doctor told her to take some time off. "Avoid stress," he said. This trip was a big deal for her. Our first vacation together, ever. And even then it wasn't really ours—it was courtesy of Liza.

We look a lot alike, and sometimes people think she's my older sister. If they really knew her, they'd think I was the older one. We both have long blond hair (mine's natural) and large blue eyes. I'm sixteen, and Shirl's forty-two.

The flight attendant took our dishes away, so everyone tried to get comfy and catch some Zzzzzs. I knew I should try since I was about to lose six hours of my life. It was 9:00 p.m. Chicago time, but 3:00 a.m. in London! But how could I sleep? English is my favorite and best subject, and soon I'd be in the land of Dickens, Shakespeare, Peter Rabbit, Sherlock Holmes, Paddington, Agatha Christie, Jane Austen, Winnie the Pooh . . .

I drifted off, still tasting asparagus, and all at once the flight attendant was serving breakfast. *Fresh seasonal fruit with warm muffins.*

Sleep. All I wanted was sleep, but it was eight in the morning on the ground below—endless miles of green patchwork quilts—a folktale illustration. Soon, we'd be arriving at London's Heathrow Airport.

The flight attendant handed us cards to fill out. Cards for "Aliens." Aliens? Like from Mars? Then it hit me. The land below was not a foreign country. No, we were the foreigners.

I looked at Dennis. Surely he'd show some sign of interest. His hands were shaking. Probably needed a cigarette. "Not much longer now," I said. He smiled at me. Amazing!

A good thing I hadn't shared with anyone the fantasy I'd concocted before we met. He'd be this great-looking guy who'd share my interests exactly. All would be happily ever after. One look at him had smashed the Prince Charming notion. I strike out like that all the time. My last boyfriend was over a year ago. It took a whole month to realize we had nothing in common. We parted by mutual consent.

The friendly blue skies soon became gray mist. Terrific. Our first sight of London would be through rain. Customs wasn't bad. I thought we'd have to swear not to bomb buses and things like that, but they just wanted to know where we'd be staying, when we'd be leaving, and if anyone had given us a package to deliver. They didn't even peek in our suitcases. I was almost disappointed. We could be spies or assassins for all they knew.

Fortunately, Shirl and Liza had exchanged American dollars for British pounds before leaving home. We were about to call a cab to take us to our hotel, when two things occurred to us: 1. We didn't have any change. 2. We didn't know how to use a British phone.

Then the miracle happened.

"Look," Dennis said.

There, among the throngs of cab drivers holding signs for the wise passengers who'd ordered their rides ahead of time, stood a man holding a card with words in large print: AMES/SULLIVAN.

"We didn't order a cab," Liza said.

"Could be a coincidence," Shirl said.

Dennis growled. "I don't care. Those are our names."

Liza approached the driver. "Excuse me, do you know who ordered this cab?"

The man answered in an odd accent, not British like you'd expect. "All I know, it's for Ames and Sullivan, party of four, coming from Chicago on flight 455."

"That's us," Shirl cried. "Fiffy must have ordered it. Let's go!"

We followed the driver to his car. We'd expected a large black bug like the other cabs, but this one was medium and gray. "Must be a private company," Shirl said.

Another passenger was in the front seat, which left the back for us. Liza and Dennis had window seats, and Shirl and I were sandwiched in between. We were totally scrunched. I sat next to Dennis, whose hands still shook. I wondered how much longer he could hold out for a cigarette.

Our driver made his way onto the "wrong side" of the highway. I yawned. He could drive down the middle for all I cared. I rested my head on Shirl's shoulder, dozing off, when I felt a sharp elbow jab my right side.

Indignant, I opened my eyes and was about to give Dennis a sharper poke in return, but he held a finger to his lips and motioned out the window. A sign pointed the way to London.

We were going in the opposite direction.

*J*eanie *placed her ear against* the bedroom door and listened to her parents arguing in the next room.

"They must not see you," her father insisted.

Her mother gave a nervous laugh. "They're probably harmless. I'm sure I've been making a big fuss over nothing. They'll just say hello and go away again."

"You don't know that. No, it isn't safe."

Jeanie returned to her bed. What wasn't safe? Who didn't they want to see? Jeanie tossed and turned through the night.

Chapter Two

NERVOUSLY, I SPOKE TO THE driver. "That sign back there. Is this the right way to London?"

"Short cut," he said curtly.

For the first time, the passenger in the front seat turned around and smiled. He was movie-star handsome—black hair streaked with silver, warm brown eyes, too-white teeth—and, when he spoke, obviously British. "Cabbie is going to my place first. Actually, you'll make better time to your hotel this way. You'll avoid much of the traffic."

This made sense. I settled back, and Shirl patted my hand.

Dennis studied a map he'd pulled out of his notebook. Then he whispered in my ear. "Our hotel is in the center of London. He can't avoid traffic."

I shrugged. One elbow jab after hours of silence did not make us best buddies. "He knows what he's doing," I whispered back. Dennis returned to his notebook and his map.

I half slept and half listened to Shirl and Liza talking with the good-looking stranger—not a movie star but an insurance salesman going home to visit his Mum for a few days. Good, he wasn't married. I spend more time fantasizing about a love life for Shirl than I do about a boyfriend for me. Not that Shirl and I weren't happy, the two of us, but the right stepfather would be nice. Maybe Shirl wouldn't have to work so hard, and we could afford to pay for our own vacations. I didn't know how much of this trip Liza had paid for, but I guess I didn't want to know, either.

The man, who introduced himself as Mr. Kent (Hey, Superman!) asked a question. "Will you spend all of your holiday in London?"

Holiday. I like that. It sounds more special than vacation.

"It depends," Liza said. "An old friend of ours from college is giving a lecture tomorrow. Perhaps you've heard of her? Dr. Fiona Douglas?"

Mr. Kent shook his head politely.

Liza continued. "Afterward, we'd like to travel around with her, if she's free. See England and Scotland, get caught up with everything. You know."

"We'll stay about two weeks," Shirl added.

Mr. Kent recited a long list of must-see places, and I started to fade out again. We all must have slept, how long I wasn't sure at first, for when I awoke, I'd lost any sense of time. Shirl and Liza were still asleep.

Dennis yawned and tried, unsuccessfully, to stretch his legs in the cramped space. He opened his map again. The compulsive type, I figured. He jabbed me, more gently this time, before pointing to a sign along the highway and to the map.

He was right! We were far from London! The sign indicated we were heading toward . . . Bath? That didn't make sense. I opened my mouth to object, but Dennis put his finger to his mouth. He wrote, "Quiet. Don't trust them," and continued to make notes.

I kept my mouth shut. I'd begun to share his suspicions. It was almost noon, and our plane had landed at 8:30. I closed Dennis's notebook when I noticed the driver watching us from the rear-view mirror. "I don't see how you can read in the car," I said loudly—for the driver's benefit and to awaken Shirl and Liza.

Dennis caught on. "Thought it might help keep me awake," he said. "This ride is taking forever."

Shirl looked at her watch and pointed out the time to Liza.

Mr. Kent laughed. "Young people are impatient, no matter what side of the pond they're on. We'll reach Mum's cottage soon. Then you'll be no more than ten minutes away from your hotel."

Shirl and Liza laughed, too, completely taken in by Mr. Kent, who no longer seemed charming to me.

"That's good," I said, pretending to believe him. Dennis gave me another elbow dig, but I'd stopped resenting what had become our safest form of communication.

Finally, the driver turned off the highway and made several turns before heading down a country road lined with thick woods on both sides. Where were we?

"Almost there," Mr. Kent told Shirl and Liza, who were raving about the beauty of the English countryside.

The driver stopped in front of a tiny cottage that was more shabby than quaint but, oddly enough, didn't look very old. "Home Sweet Home." Mr. Kent opened the passenger door and got out. "Do come in for a cup of tea. Mum would be delighted to meet you."

For the first time, Shirl looked uncomfortable. "How kind of you, but we should go to our hotel. This has taken a lot longer than I anticipated."

"Perhaps we'll meet again," Liza added.

I waited, feeling Dennis's tension as well as my own. Were we wrong about Mr. Kent?

Unfortunately, no. He opened the door on Liza's side. "I'm afraid I must insist." He pointed a small but efficient-looking pistol at us. "Get out and take your belongings with you. Cabbie, bring in their luggage."

Shirl and Liza gasped, Dennis and I remained quiet, but we all did as he asked.

Mr. Kent unlocked the cottage door, motioning us into a surprisingly large room containing a sofa, a table, and four cots made up. We were expected.

"Where's your mother?" Apparently, Shirl wasn't ready to give up on Mr. Kent. He was handsome.

No more charming smile. Instead, he sneered at her. "Alas, Mum is dead, but you needn't worry you'll be joining her. You're in no danger as long as you do as you're told. Make yourselves comfortable. The toilet is in the other room, although I'm afraid there's no water. That and your food should arrive later." He tipped an imaginary hat. "Ladies, gentleman, this has been a pleasure. You've made it quite easy. I trust we won't meet again." And he left the cottage.

We stared at the door, stunned. Dennis tried to open it. Locked, of course. Then he began banging on it. "Let us out of here!"

"Let's see if there's another way out," I cried.

We rushed into the bathroom. Only one high window with frosted panes, too small to fit through. Back in the living room, the only window was also too high to reach, so Dennis and I pushed the table next to the wall and climbed up. While Liza and Shirl pleaded that we be careful, Dennis and I looked out.

Mr. Kent stood alone. He lifted his arm as if he were signaling. Two men came out of the woods and shook hands with him before he walked off into the woods. One of the men ambled over to a stump across from the cottage and sat watching. The other man left, maybe to keep guard in back.

I got off the table. "Might as well face facts. We've been kidnapped."

"Kidnapped?" Liza said. "Why would anyone kidnap us?"

"I don't know, but it looks like your friend Fiona is responsible—if she sent the car."

Liza shook her head. "I'm trying to remember. I don't believe I did send the flight information. I just said we'd be coming."

Shirl started to cry, probably from fatigue as much as fear. But I remembered her doctor's warning. For avoiding stress, we were off to a bad start.

Dennis opened his notebook again. "What are you doing?" I said. "Shouldn't we try to get out of here?"

"I got the license number, but I need to make sketches of the men while I still remember what they look like. Nothing else to do now. Those two thugs aren't going to let us go anywhere. You can bet they've got guns, too."

"I didn't think English people carried guns." Dennis didn't respond to my stupid comment.

While Shirl rested on a cot and Liza searched the cupboards for anything that might help, I watched Dennis sketch the driver, Mr. Kent, and the guard. It was magical watching his pencil move around the paper. "One more look," he said, and climbed onto the table again.

"Dennis knew something was wrong hours ago. He clued me in, but we didn't know how to tell you." I handed Liza the notebook—really a sketchpad. "Look, he wrote down the license number of the cab and made sketches of Mr. Kent and the men."

Liza smiled. I got the feeling she wasn't used to being proud of him.

Dennis seemed embarrassed by my praise. As soon as he got off the table, he retrieved the sketchpad and added a few lines to his sketch. "Now we'll have something to show the police when we get out of here."

"If we get out of here," Shirl said.

"If they were going to hurt us, they would have done it already."

Dennis nodded. "I agree with Carly. I can't believe they didn't take anything—money, traveler's checks, credit cards, our passports."

"What will we do?" Liza gave each of us a bewildered look.

"For the moment, nothing," Dennis said. "We're too tired. We might as well do what Mr. Kent said—make ourselves comfortable."

No one spoke. Each of us claimed a cot. We closed our eyes.

*J*eanie joined her parents for tea.

"I took care of everything," her father said. "You won't see them."

"What did you do?" Jeanie's mother sounded afraid.

Her father laughed. "Nothing to worry about. I just gave them a wee taste of British country life."

Jeanie toyed with her scone. Somehow she knew not to ask questions.

Chapter Three

M Y HEART FLEW TO MY throat. I clutched my blanket in the dark, listening. Certain the kidnappers had returned. I heard voices, clicks, scuffling noises—and then nothing. Gradually, I fell back asleep until I was awakened again, this time by daylight.

Had I dreamed the nighttime noises? I dashed to the door, which opened easily. Not a dream. No more locks, no more guards. I looked out at the woods. Twenty-four hours ago, I'd marveled at all the greenness. Now, I'd cheerfully substitute skyscrapers and exhaust fumes. We might be free, but free to do what?

"Wake up, everyone. They're gone. Let's get out of here!"

Shirl, who wakes up the way I do, quickly, joined me. Liza and Dennis groaned and turned over on their cots while we sat outside on the front stoop.

"I can hardly believe it happened," she said, her voice trembling, "but here we are."

I kept my words light, even though I didn't feel so light inside. "That's right. Snatched and plunked right down in Winnie the Pooh's Hundred Acres Woods."

"Do you think they'll come back again?"

I shook my head. "I don't think they'd have unlocked the door if they were."

A loud demanding snore from inside made us jump. We both giggled.

"That's Liza," Shirl said. "She snored like that in college, all four years."

"How did you stand it?"

Shirl smiled. "Because I love her. She's the most generous person I know—not just with money. I don't suppose her snores were any worse than me banging drawers before sunrise, looking for something I'd lost."

"You still do that." I gave her a hug.

Liza and Dennis finally got up. Not exactly morning people. Both looked like they'd been to some wild party where they'd had too much to drink.

Something in the room was different—a small picnic basket and bottles had appeared on the table. "They did come inside last night!" We headed for the water before we talked again.

"Now for food," Liza said.

"Probably drugged," Dennis said.

Liza took inventory: sealed packages of scones, small wrapped pats of butter, a few barely ripe bananas, small cartons of orange juice, a box of milk, and paper cups. "No coffee," she wailed.

While eating, we talked about the mess we were in. We might be free, but we didn't have a clue where we were. "The last sign before we turned off the highway pointed to Bath," Dennis said. "That's where we should go."

"How?" Liza buttered another scone.

I had an idea. "Let's walk into the woods where we saw Mr. Kent leave. He must have gone somewhere."

"Logical," Dennis said.

"Walk?" Liza wailed again. "But we'll have to carry all this luggage."

"Would you prefer to spend our vacation here and not see Fiona at all?" Shirl asked gently.

Liza flushed. "Sorry. I just don't see why they couldn't have left a thermos of coffee."

We were about to leave when we heard the honking of a car horn. Now what? Out front, we saw a fat black cab and its driver, standing next to it.

"He looks as confused as we do," I said. "Let's chance it."

"You the ones wanted a cab?" The driver seemed less anxious as we approached him.

"Yes," Liza said, reaching for the door handle.

Dennis grabbed her arm. "That depends," he said to the driver. "Who sent you?"

"Don't know, guv. My orders were to pick up four people at a cabin near Limpley Stoke who needed transport to Bath. Some bloke wired over the directions and coach tickets to London." We looked at each other and nodded slowly. What choice did we have? It was go with the driver or take a walk into the unknown.

"Write down the license number and make a sketch of the driver," I whispered to Dennis.

"Count on it," he said.

While Dennis and the cab driver loaded the suitcases, I talked with Shirl and Liza. "We should go straight to the Bath police."

"Can't that wait until London?" Liza asked. "We still might be in time to see Fiona."

"I agree," Shirl said. "Besides, nothing really bad happened. I can't believe Mr. Kent meant us any harm. He was charming . . . most of the time."

"Charming, Shirl? He locked us into a cabin—at gunpoint."

"I agree with Mom." Dennis joined us. "Let's wait until London. I'm not sure the cops will believe us anyway. Kidnappers who provide a cottage, food, a cab, and bus tickets? Remember, they didn't take anything."

Except our time, I thought. "I think you're all wrong," I said reluctantly, "but okay, we'll wait until London. But this isn't over. If Scotland Yard doesn't believe us, we'll go to the American Embassy."

Our driver cleared his throat, looking at his watch. We all climbed into the back seat. Plenty of room At least we'd be comfortable this time. The driver handed Liza the bus tickets. "Bought four days ago," she said, looking them over.

"Part of the plan," I muttered.

"What time does the bus leave?" Dennis asked.

Liza read off the ticket. "13:30."

"Translated, that's 1:30," I said. "We'll miss Fiona's lecture."

The trip to Bath took about twenty minutes. The driver tore through the congested streets like a stock car racer on his day off. I had an idea. "Could you drive us straight through to London?" What was I thinking? Probably cost as much as a plane ticket.

"Oh no, miss," he said. "I have my fares arranged for this afternoon. Wouldn't be right to them, you know."

Liza smiled at me. "Don't worry, Carly. We'll track down Fiona somehow. We've come too far to give up now."

A thought had started to push through from the back of my brain. Although I wasn't able to put it into words yet, I knew I wanted Liza to stop talking. I looked at the driver to see if he'd reacted to what she'd said about finding Fiona. No, he seemed to be concentrating on keeping tourists from crossing the street and on the song he was singing, something about roaming on the bonnie banks of Clyde.

I took a peek at Dennis's sketchbook but didn't understand much. Some notes, some lines that looked like noses and eyebrows. He worked frantically every time the cab stopped at a traffic light. I decided he was a genius. Unpleasant, but a genius.

Our cab pulled into the bus station. Liza opened her purse and pulled out her wallet. "Oh no, madam. Your fare has been paid."

"How thoughtful," Shirl said sarcastically. "Could we offer you a tip?"

The driver nodded, smiling.

"How much?" she and Liza mouthed to each other. Liza pulled out a wad of bills. I'd studied the money before we left home and pointed to a five-pound note. Should be enough. I had the feeling he'd already been paid well. The look on his face when Liza gave him the tip confirmed this. Smug.

We stood with our suitcases on the sidewalk of a busy circle, surrounded by people waiting for or getting on and off guide buses, coaches, and cabs. It was 11:00. Our bus wouldn't leave for over two hours.

"Maybe we can exchange these tickets for an earlier bus," Liza said. "Wait here a second." She walked off and started talking to someone who looked like it was his job to help anxious tourists. I could see him examining the tickets.

All at once, I wasn't in such a hurry to leave. I mean, here we were—in Bath. I wanted to see it. Not just the Roman stuff. Jane Austen once lived here, and almost all her characters either loved or hated it. Was our whole vacation going to be about Fiffy, who didn't seem interested in us?

Liza came back, shaking her head. "No exchange on the tickets, and the earlier coaches to London are full. We can put our bags in lockers, though, and our tickets entitle us to a free tour of the town." She pointed to Guide Friday, a two-story, open-air bus.

"Wonderful," Shirl said. "And we'll get you a cup of coffee to take along."

I rebelled. "Please, Shirl. I've been sitting practically since we left Chicago. I'd like to see Bath on foot."

"Not a good idea, Carly. We should stay together."

"The bus tour is a better plan, although a break from each other would be pleasant," Liza said. Did she need a break from Dennis or me?

Dennis came to the rescue. "I'll go with Carly. I'm sure we'll be safe as long as we're together. It's sure to be crowded. No one would dare try anything."

Liza nodded. "We'll meet you back here. How long is the tour?"

We checked. Just an hour. We got some change for the lockers and coffee for Liza. Dennis and I watched them board the bus. Shirl still looked uncertain, but she waved. "Be careful, Carly. Don't . . ."

". . . take rides from strangers," I called back.

Finally, she grinned and blew me a kiss. The tour guide blasted through the loudspeaker and the bus pulled out.

Dennis turned to me. "Where to?"

*J*eanie *winced as Nanny drove* a comb through her tangled sand-colored curls. "Ouch, Nan. Do stop, please."

Nanny proceeded more gently with the hairbrush. "Sorry, luv. Your hair has its own mind as to what's proper."

Jeanie examined her new green dress and neat hair-do in the full-length mirror. Properly uncomfortable—that's how she looked.

Silly that she had to go hear Mum speak; she wouldn't understand a word. But Pops said this was a great honour for Mum, that everyone expected her to be there.

Jeanie didn't care about everyone, but she did care about Mum, who looked happier today. So did Pops. They smiled a lot and said everything would be fine.

For Jeanie, the fine part was going home. Tonight, right after the reception, they would board the InterCity train at Euston Station and go home. Home to Scotland.

Chapter Four

WITH ONLY AN HOUR BEFORE Guide Friday returned, we didn't have time for much. "The Roman Baths," I said. "That's where to."

We left the bus station, heading up Manvers Street, where the first thing we saw was the police station. Could it be one of those meaningful coincidences we'd talked about in philosophy class? I knew we should go in. The Moms and Dennis had their little reasons why we shouldn't, but they were wrong. Kidnapping is serious. The only reason for not reporting your own kidnapping is because you're still a captive, for heaven's sake!

I thought over what Dennis had said about no one believing us. Without Liza and Shirl along, he might be right. I mean, the way the two of us looked—like Alice in Wonderland and the Beast from 40 Fathoms. Oh, well, standing in the bright sunshine in this lovely old town, even I could hardly believe it. Regretfully, I gave a mental farewell to the police station. London it would have to be.

Bath is a terrific place for tourists. Signs with little arrows point to the sights on practically every corner, just about everything in walking distance. "Feels good to walk, doesn't it?" Dennis asked, as we turned onto the old North Parade Passage, following the sign to Bath Abbey and Roman Baths.

"Sure does." I saw my chance to ask Dennis—"Don't you want a cigarette? Now that your mom isn't around?"

Dennis turned red. "How did you know I smoked?"

"Are you kidding? You reeked when I first met you."

"I guess I overdid it before we left home," he confessed. "They were the last ones I'll ever have. I quit."

"Right," I said sarcastically. I knew kids at school who were always saying the same thing. None of them stuck to it much more than a day.

"No, really. My dad said if I quit smoking this summer, he'd give me a car on my next birthday. Not bad, huh?"

I turned on him. "You mean you're going to get a reward for not wrecking your body?"

Dennis looked smug. "Yep, parents are funny that way."

"Not mine. If I smoked, Shirl would take away my allowance or lock me in my room. Probably both."

"Well, don't get excited. Families are different. I've been meaning to quit anyway. The car is just great motivation."

We didn't talk for a while—just kept walking, passing by quaint shops and one little pinkish-colored restaurant with three stories ending in a high-peaked roof. Outside each window, red geraniums nestled in stencil-covered window boxes. I read the sign. "Sally Lunn's, The Oldest House in Bath." I wanted to find out about Sally Lunn. Maybe we could come back for lunch.

"Hey, Carly, don't stay mad," Dennis said, interrupting my plans.

"Sorry, I'm not really. You're right—families are different. I'm just sensitive about smoking. You know, since my father died of lung cancer."

He seemed surprised. "I didn't know that."

I was surprised, too. "Shirl talks about all of you. Doesn't your mother talk about us?"

"We don't talk much, about anything," he said.

We turned a corner and reached our destination—a large pedestrian area called Abbey Square, and it was like we weren't in England anymore. On one side of the square, the mighty gothic cathedral, Bath Abbey, looked British enough, but the rest reminded me of pictures I'd seen of ancient Rome. Columns in different styles marched along the fronts of stone buildings.

We joined the long line (queue in England) in front of a narrow doorway marked Roman Baths. It would be too bad if we spent the whole hour waiting to get inside. But the queue moved quickly, and soon we could see the ticket booth.

"Oh, shit!" Dennis said loudly.

"What's wrong?" I whispered, trying to ignore the people staring disapproval at us.

"Mom forgot to give me English money. I've just got American."

"Is that all? I'll loan you the money. You can pay me back." Fortunately, Shirl didn't believe in keeping all our money in one place and had turned quite a bit over to me. I pulled a ten-pound note from my wallet, five for each of us, and another two pounds to buy a guide book. I like to know what I'm seeing. Dennis was still embarrassed. "Look, Dennis, forget it. Shirl and I wouldn't even be here if it weren't for your parents. And if we hadn't been kidnapped, you'd have British money by now."

"I doubt it. Mom doesn't trust me much with money." He sounded bitter, but he smiled at me. I was starting to like his smile.

We walked from exhibit to exhibit, heading toward the Great Roman Bath. I'm not fond of crowds, but this one was different— respectful and in awe. As I watched the eerie light filtering through the sacred-spring waterfall feeding the bath, I was ready to believe in the goddess Minerva myself. I stared at the bronze head of the goddess and thought about the many people who had worshiped her throughout the centuries.

The crowds had thinned out by the time we reached the open courtyard of the Great Bath. We sat on a stone bench where we could look over the columns and see the towers of Bath Abbey. Great atmosphere, but Dennis broke the spell by reading from the guidebook. "Listen to this, Carly. If I were around in those days, I'd have been oiled and scraped before I could take a bath. Scraped! And there'd be jugglers and servants and all sorts of people watching me."

He laughed, and I started to giggle. "Not a pretty sight." I stood, stretching. We should move on. But I took only two steps. Mr. Kent! Ducking behind a column! Did he know I'd seen him? I didn't think so. I took a deep breath. No time for fear. Grabbing Dennis's arm, I spoke in an undertone. "Dennis, play along with me. No matter what I say, go along with it." He looked puzzled but nodded.

I led Dennis over to the column where I'd seen Mr. Kent, hoping he was still there, hiding. I wanted him to hear. "Too bad we can't stay all day, but it's time to meet Shirl and Liza. Then let's go back to that cute little restaurant we saw—Sally Lunn's—and just hang out there and people-watch until we have to get the bus for London." Man, did I sound phony. Would it work?

Dennis made a face but said the right words. "Fine, Carly, whatever you say. After all, you're paying." He sounded as phony as I.

We hurried from the courtyard and out the building. I would have liked to stop at the Pump Room to sample a drink of the sacred water—even if it's supposed to taste disgusting—but it appeared that Mr. Kent was still in charge of our "holiday."

As soon as we reached the square, Dennis started. "What's going on? We don't have to meet the bus yet."

"Keep walking." I looked over my shoulder. "I don't think anyone's following us now."

"Following? What do you mean?"

"Mr. Kent."

"What? Where?"

"Shhh! He was hiding behind a column. That's why I led you over there and said all that nonsense—so he'd think we were sticking to his plan to use the tickets. So he wouldn't think he had to follow us anymore."

Dennis gave a nervous grin. "That's why you said we'd be watching people at the restaurant. He'd know we'd be sure to spot him, too."

"Do you think it worked?"

He shrugged. "Hard to tell. So if we're not going to the bus station, where are we going?"

"The police station. Right this minute."

Impressive words, and I meant them. I think I expected the bobbies would stop everything and run out and arrest Mr. Kent. What actually happened at the Manvers Street Station was another long queue. The people standing in front of us were practically coming to blows about a car accident.

"Didn't you see me, man? I was the only one in the round about."

"Oh, right, you think yer the only one. Think you own the whole bloomin' street."

The people in front of them were hot, too. "We'll miss our train to London."

"Oh, hush," someone said. "Take another one. They leave every quarter hour."

I pulled Dennis out of line and back onto the street. "Are you crazy?" he said.

"Possibly, but I've got another idea. It will take hours to see a policeman, and we've got to meet Shirl and Liza. What if Mr. Kent didn't buy my act and goes to the bus station?"

"So, what's your idea?"

"The train. Didn't you hear? One leaves for London every fifteen minutes. For some reason, Mr. Kent wants us to take the bus. Let's stop being his puppets."

Dennis nodded. "About time we changed the rules. One of us should buy tickets. Do you have enough money?"

"I think so. I'll go, and you wait for the bus."

Dennis agreed. We were working as a team now. "Get us some lockers, too. As soon as you get back, I'll start hauling over the suitcases."

I gave Dennis some money for a soda and took off for Bath Spa Railway Station. If I just kept moving and planning, I wouldn't have time to think about how scared I was.

*A*s soon as *Jeanie and* Pops were introduced and the applause died down, Mum began to talk, and Jeanie opened her new book, *The Chalet Girls in Camp.* Pops bought her a new Chalet School book every time she had to attend one of Mum's lectures, and it made going quite bearable. Jeanie had longed to read this volume, for the back cover said Joey, her favourite of the Chalet girls, was going to mysteriously disappear. The Chalet girls had such exciting times. Jeanie wanted to go away to school someday, too. Mum said she could. Jeanie would have roommates and adventures—all the things Mum said she'd always wanted but never had.

Chapter Five

MISSION ACCOMPLISHED. WE FOUR WERE whizzing along on BritRail's InterCity, heading toward Paddington Station, and I felt like I had earned back some of my self-respect. So much for you, Mr. Kent. Go kidnap someone else—buy them bus tickets. We won't be your victims anymore.

Luckily, Shirl and Liza had caught on quickly to the situation. Our train ride would take an hour and twenty minutes. We had a chance, barely, of getting to the lecture hall before Fiona finished speaking.

We sat facing each other—Dennis and me across from Shirl and Liza, with a table in between. Dennis returned to his ever-present sketchbook, Liza slept, and Shirl opened the copy of Jane Austen's *Northanger Abbey* she'd bought in Bath Spa Station. I examined my purchased treasures: postcards, a geological survey map of "Bath and Environs," and a blank notebook. I'd bought the map because I decided we should try to pinpoint the location of our prison-cottage and the notebook to see if I could use words, like Dennis used pictures, to make sense of what had happened to us.

I opened to the first page. How to start? The page was as blank as my mind had become. I stared out the window at the villages rushing past. No, try harder. What if I made a list? I wrote *Things to Find Out* and began:

1. *Why were we kidnapped?*
2. *Where were we taken?*
3. *Who is Mr. Kent?*
4. *Who was Sally Lunn?*

I don't know why I wrote that last question except I was frustrated we weren't stopping for the sights along the way. I was acquiring an unreasonable dislike of Fiona. Finally, the pen and I warmed up. *Carly's Journal: A Record of a Kidnapping*, I wrote decisively, and began: *The whole thing started about six months ago when I was seated in the dental hygienist's chair . . .*

I wrote non-stop for about forty minutes when the thought percolating in the back of my brain since morning formed into words on the page. *Mr. Kent, or someone who hired him, doesn't want us to go to Fiona Douglas's lecture.* It was as simple or as complicated as that, for the only thing taken from us was time—the time needed to be in London for Fiffy's appearance.

Excited, I looked over at Dennis, wanting to talk it over with him without the Moms, as I now dubbed them. He might have felt my eyes on him, for he closed his sketchbook and stood up. "I'm hungry," he said. "Anyone else?" Shirl offered to accompany him to the buffet car (pronounced "boofy" in England) to fetch sandwiches for all of us. Liza still slept. I'd stay behind and watch our stuff.

Actually, I had an ulterior motive for staying. As soon as Shirl and Dennis opened the door into the next car, I grabbed Dennis's sketchbook. From the first page, it was a picture diary of our trip: the Moms hugging at the airport, our jet heading into the clouds, the flight attendant serving roasted nuts and orange juice. I was delighted—until I reached the first drawing of me.

Dennis had sketched the two of us seated in the airplane. While he had over-emphasized his poor appearance, he had also made himself look shy and vulnerable, totally at the mercy of the creature seated next to him. Was this how Dennis saw me? Mouth pursed in disapproval, nose tilted and nostrils pinched as if detecting a bad smell, eyelids slightly closed, eyebrows coming together in a frown. Dennis had highlighted my long hair, giving the illusion of a little-girl bow, or perhaps a halo. My face burned, and I checked to see that Liza hadn't awakened. While I was certain I hadn't looked like that, he'd captured how I'd felt, exactly.

I flipped through more pages—the bogus cab driver, Mr. Kent, the guard, the real taxi driver, a sketch of the two cars complete with license numbers. More sketches of me—sitting on the stone bench in the Roman Bath, laughing, standing next to the column with fear in my eyes, looking frazzled in the queue at the police station and, finally, sitting calmly in the train writing in my journal. The newer sketches portrayed me more as I saw myself. Obviously, Dennis's opinion had changed.

"Don't let him catch you with that." Startled, I closed the book and looked up to see Liza, wide awake. "Frightening, isn't it? How he captures feelings as well as appearances?"

I shoved the journal back where it belonged. "He's terrific."

Liza made a face. "That's the problem. It's all he wants to do—draw, for a living someday, I mean. But his father won't hear of it."

I felt a surge of gratitude for Shirl, who has always allowed me to be me. "What's wrong with that? I'll bet he could find plenty of work. He could get a job as a police sketch artist."

Liza burst out laughing, but it was a bitter laugh. "Dennis working *for* the police? Now, wouldn't that be a change?"

Shirl and Dennis returned then with our food. I didn't think they'd overheard Liza's comment. At least, I hoped they hadn't.

The minute I bit into my egg and cress sandwich, nothing else mattered. None of us had eaten anything since our picnic breakfast hours before. Next came the bag of chips—crisps I should say— washed down with a warm Pepsi. Time for dessert. "Great cookies," I told Dennis.

He smiled that super ear-to-ear smile of his. "You mean 'biscuits.'" I guessed he hadn't heard his mother's nasty remark.

The view from the window was changing. No more quaint villages and stretches of green. Everything about us spelled C-I-T-Y, an industrial one. We became aware of the other passengers in our car. It had been a quiet trip. But now they began to throw their trash into little bins provided in the aisles and to gather their luggage. They were the experts, and we imitated them. The train stopped, and one of the passengers opened the door. In good order, we all filed out.

My first impression of Paddington Station was heat and fumes. Dennis found a large luggage trolley. We loaded our belongings, beginning the long trek into the great shell of a station.

"We've got to find a taxi, fast," Liza insisted, studying the signs overhead. "It might not be too late. Fiffy still could be speaking."

"Wouldn't she wait for you?" I asked.

They ignored me and kept reading the signs. But I wanted to look around the station. Of course I knew I wouldn't really find a bear. Still . . . "Oh, there's a stall that sells stuffed Paddingtons," I said. "Couldn't we stop so I can buy one?"

Liza gave me a look that said clearly, "Grow up!" Her actual words were, "I'm sure you can find those bears all over London."

She didn't get it. No one did. Buying it somewhere else wouldn't count. We worked our way out of the station onto a busy street, where, amazingly, Dennis managed to hail a cab. Liza gave the address of the university, and we were on our way.

I felt annoyed. And misunderstood. I opened my journal and turned to a new page. *Things I Want to Do*, I wrote, as peevishly as a small child.

1. *Go to Bath – taste the water.*
2. *Eat lunch at Sally Lunn's.*
3. *Buy a bear at Paddington Station.*

*R*eluctantly, *Jeanie closed her book* as the approving applause took her out of Joey's world. She'd read later in the train, she silently promised Joey.

Everyone stood for Mum, so Jeanie did, too. Some people had tears in their eyes. That always happened after Mum's speeches. Jeanie didn't understand why Mum always talked about sad things. The clapping was so loud Jeanie almost didn't hear Pops's mobile phone ringing. She gave him a nudge and pointed to his pocket.

"I'll have to take this," Pops mouthed. "You stay here."

Jeanie should have stayed, but instead she followed Pops out into the hall and stood quietly behind him.

"What do you mean you lost them? Look, Kent, you took the assignment. Find them if you expect to be paid."

Kent. That would be Mr. Travis. Jeanie didn't like Mr. Travis. He had a strange smile—just teeth flashing, not a real smile at all.

Pops ended the call. He didn't turn around and see Jeanie, but she could tell he was angry. He was still—and so stiff. "Fiona," he said. "I've got to get Fiona out of here."

Jeanie tiptoed back to her seat, where she wished she'd waited.

Chapter Six

THE MOMS' VISION OF A quick dash over to the university faded as reality took over. One does not dash through the streets of London. I stared out the window, fascinated. How does anyone ever learn this city? It didn't seem to have any plan. Streets wound around every which way, forming circles and squares, veering off at sharp angles. I hoped Londoners appreciated their bus and taxi drivers.

While we hadn't reached the sites of major tourist attractions, occasionally we saw something we recognized from movies: red telephone booths, old-fashioned postboxes, double-decker buses, horse-drawn carriages in a park.

"Hyde Park," reported our resident sketcher and map reader, Dennis Ames. "Look, we're going to pass right near our hotel. Let's stop and leave the suitcases. Then we won't have to lug them around the university."

Shirl objected. "But we'll lose so much time."

"Maybe not," said Liza, who, Dennis had told me, tries to get out of carrying her usual ton of luggage whenever possible. "Good idea, Dennis." Dennis looked startled but pleased.

"Why don't we stick to our plan and have the driver take our bags back to the hotel without us?" Shirl said.

The three of us turned on her and glared. "Honestly, Shirl," Liza said, "haven't you learned anything?"

Liza told the driver about our change in plans, and after conquering a few disorganized blocks, our car pulled up in front of Grosvenor House—not exactly the quaint, no-star establishment I'd pictured. Liza had told us the hotel was nicknamed "The Old Lady of Park Lane," but I hadn't expected such an elegant lady. Could we afford to stay here? "Liza, this can't be the right hotel."

She gave me an understanding smile. "Don't worry, dear. The manager owes Mr. Ames a few favors."

"Okay, thanks," I said quietly. Shirl and I were not used to such a formal place. She and I waited with the driver while Liza and Dennis followed our luggage to the registration desk. They returned quickly, looking bewildered.

"What happened?" Shirl asked, as the driver forged his way back into battle.

"Someone changed our reservations," Liza explained. "A man called the hotel claiming to be my husband and cancelled last night's booking. He even offered to pay for it, but the desk clerk told him it wasn't necessary."

"Too bad," Dennis said. "We might have traced him."

Should I say what was on my mind? I proceeded cautiously. "I hate to say this, since she's your friend, but everything that's happened to us must be connected with Fiona. Who else even knew where we'd be staying?"

"Oh, I'm sure I must have told people," Liza said vaguely.

Shirl, although a charter member of the Fiona Fan Club, supported me. "Carly may be right. Let's not tell anyone what happened until we talk to the police."

"Scotland Yard," I added for emphasis. "Let's go there right after we see Fiona." That should have been our first stop, but I had been outvoted.

"Quiet, everyone," Dennis insisted. "Look what you're missing."

London! No doubt about it. Trafalgar Square. Nelson's Column. Parents trying to keep their children off the lions and out of the fountains. And pigeons strutting everywhere. I wanted to jump out of the cab and give greetings and breadcrumbs to each one. I saw the National Gallery and, in the distance, the Admiralty Arch, proclaiming the entrance to one of the most famous roads in the world. But would we take the route leading to Buckingham Palace? No! I sighed.

"We'll come back soon, Carly. First thing, I promise."

I smiled, relieved by Shirl's words. The rest of the ride seemed like a movie—the houses of Parliament, Big Ben, the river Thames . . . All at once, I changed my mind about Fiona. I couldn't wait to meet her. After all, she was the reason we'd come to London. She must be wonderful if Shirl and Liza still cared about her after so many years. I didn't even know how she looked, other than she was very short and acted more Spanish than British. Shirl has pictures of everyone but her. Fiffy hated to be photographed. Shirl said she even pretended to be sick whenever yearbook photos were taken.

We turned down a quiet lane, following a discreet sign leading to the university. The Moms grew more and more excited. They held hands and grinned at each other. I hoped they wouldn't squeal and totally embarrass us. Our driver stopped in front of an old brownstone covered with ivy.

Inside, the somber building appeared empty. A sign perched on an easel was our only greeter. The notice advertised Dr. Douglas's lecture as being in Room 34. "We're not too late. Hurry!" Liza urged.

"I'd like to go to the bathroom first and at least try to clean up," Dennis said, pointing out two doors on our left. We stared at each other. We looked awful!

Shirl wailed. "We can't see Fiona like this!" She was right. We were still wearing the clothes we'd left home in, for we hadn't thought of changing in Limpley Stoke. Clothes weren't important then. In the train, I'd brushed my hair and splashed water on my face, but I bet I looked as bad as everyone else.

Shirl and Liza were middle-aged and frumpy, their makeup not even a memory. Frankly, Dennis looked dangerous—greasy hair, and he needed a shave. None of us spoke. We headed straight for the Ladies and Gents.

Hairbrushes and makeup revived the Moms and me, but Dennis still looked hopeless. I gave him a package of breath mints. Ready or not, time to meet Fiona.

Two-thirty, my watch said as we approached Room 34. Too quiet. The lecture couldn't be over yet. But it was. The room was empty except for a sixty-something mouse of a woman, stuffing papers into a briefcase. We rushed over to her, and she took a step back. "We've come to hear Dr. Douglas," Liza said. "All the way from the United States. Where is she?"

Liza must have come on too strong, for the mouse squeaked. "You're too late. The lecture's over." She might as well have said, "Leave, or I'll fetch the bobbies."

Shirl began to cry softly. "Oh, Fiffy, you knew we were coming. Why didn't you wait for us?"

A better approach. The woman examined Shirl closely. "Fiffy? No one has called her that since she was a girl. You must know her."

"Oh, we do," Shirl said. "We were her best friends."

"Will you help us?" Liza pleaded.

They'd won. She introduced herself as Fiona's personal secretary, Miss Grainger. "There's a little reception for her out in the courtyard," she said. "For her and the family." Family? Liza and Shirl exchanged puzzled glances.

We followed Miss Grainger through the lecture room, a short hallway, down another flight of stairs. Finally, we entered a walled garden, where fashionable-looking people were milling around sipping tea or wine. A few of them looked at us, raised their eyebrows, and turned away. I couldn't blame them.

"There she is. There's Fiona." Tears streamed down Shirl's cheeks. Then, loudly enough for everyone to hear, "Liza, it's Fiona!"

At the sound of Shirl's voice, people seemed to fade away, perhaps not wanting to be associated with loud, untidy Americans. Then I could see what Shirl had seen—a group standing in the center of the garden watching us. With the group was one of the tiniest women I'd ever seen—Fiona. She didn't approach five feet, but in her cream-colored business suit she was the last word in fashion. Her hair was a tumble of short black curls that she wore like a stylish cap. Her whole face glowed with fun and spirit. She was exactly as Shirl had described.

"Fiffy!" Liza charged forth. She gave Fiona a hug that lifted her into the air.

Fiona laughed. "Oh my, oh dear . . . Liza, how lovely, you haven't changed at all."

"Well, you have." Liza laughed, too.

Shirl hurried forward. "Shirley, how jolly." Fiona gave her a peck on the cheek and a quick hug.

Liza looked dismayed, and Shirl, hurt. But Fiona didn't seem to notice their reactions.

Dennis did. "What happened?" he whispered.

"Tell you later," I said. No wonder Shirl's feelings were hurt. Her name isn't Shirley—it's Shirl. Shirl Annette Conway, now Sullivan. Shirl is not a nickname for Shirley, and all her friends know that. How could Fiona have forgotten?

Shirl recovered quickly and introduced Dennis and me. Fiona didn't even blink at Dennis's appearance. I liked her for that. Then Fiona called some people over—an enormous bald man and an adorable little girl, about nine. "This is my husband, Torquil MacNeil."

"We had no idea you were married," Liza said, shaking Mr. MacNeil's hand.

The little girl pulled on Fiona's suit jacket and smiled at me. Here was one person who wanted to meet us. When Fiona didn't respond, the child took charge. "I'm Jean Morag Catriona MacNeil." Then she giggled. "But you can call me Jeanie. I'm Mum's daughter."

There was no doubt that by "Mum," she meant Fiona, for other than hair color, the little girl was a startling replica.

Liza whooped, that's the only word for it, and gave Jeanie one of her overdone hugs. Only I heard the moan. I turned around just in time to see Shirl sink to the ground in a dead faint.

*V*oices woke Jeanie. *She was* still in bed. They'd delayed their trip until tomorrow. Mum said they needed to be sure the lady who fainted was all right. The ladies were Mum's roommates at university. Strange, Jeanie was certain Mum had told her she'd never had roommates.

The voices grew louder. Jeanie got up and opened the door slightly. She heard Pops. "I tell you, they suspect something."

"Nonsense. They were delighted to see me."

"Then why did she faint?"

"Perhaps because you've kept them dashing about for two days without the chance to eat or rest properly."

Pops's response was muffled.

Mum went on. "I've made up my mind, Torquil. I like them, and I'm going to invite them to come home with us."

"Without considering my wishes, Fiona?"

Mum was silent for a moment. "I'm sorry, Torquil, but I have been robbed of so much. Perhaps I'll be able to make it up to myself in this small way."

"Let's wait to see how our next meeting goes, luv."

Jeanie didn't understand any of this. Boring grown-up stuff. She looked out the window at the sparkling pink lights on Albert Bridge. What fun it would be to have American visitors. She especially liked the tall dark lady who gave the super hugs and the blonde girl who looked like a fairy princess. The boy could be an American rock star. In fact, Jeanie was sure he was.

Chapter Seven

"I'M PERFECTLY FINE," SHIRL SAID the next morning, "but you three should go without me."

I began to relax. She did seem better, but I had been terrified last night. Fiona and Torquil (he asked me to call him that) had been terrific. Fiona helped revive Shirl, and Torquil called their personal London physician—sounds more important than doctor—who agreed to meet us at our hotel. Fiona and Torquil drove us back to Grosvenor House.

Being in trouble in a strange country is not fun, something we were learning the hard way. At least I liked the doctor. He scolded Shirl for not taking better care of herself but said all she really needed was rest and regular meals. Liza and I pulled him aside. "Do you think it's her heart?" Liza asked. "She's had some problems."

He shook his head but looked puzzled. "No, but she's behaving as if she'd received some sort of shock." Liza explained the whole roommates reunion thing, leaving out the kidnapping part. "It must have been all the excitement then." The doctor left his number and told us to call if Shirl hadn't improved by morning. I heard Torquil say he'd settle the bill, which I thought was beyond nice of him. Torquil and Fiona said goodnight and that we'd meet for lunch if Shirl was up to it.

Shirl slept fitfully, calling out Fiona's name a few times. I didn't sleep so well either. I kept waking up to check on her. It may not be cool to say you love your mother, but I do. Shirl's all I've got. Besides, she's pretty wonderful.

In the morning, Shirl kept telling us she was fine; we should go without her. Dennis had discovered, through his incessant map studying, that the U.S. Embassy was right up the street—on Park Lane, the same as our hotel. "Okay, Shirl," I gave in finally, "but you've got to promise to rest the whole time we're gone." Shirl promised.

The embassy was not the secretive-looking building we'd expected. Instead, it was huge, barrack-like, and almost entirely made of glass. A receptionist escorted us into a small room that had nothing in it but a table and chairs. Finally, after Dennis said, "ten more minutes and I'm oud-a-here," two men entered the room and introduced themselves as Mr. Jones and Mr. Smith from British Intelligence and Interpol. Right. Like I believed those names.

They led us through the whole story of our kidnapping. Then they made us tell it again, asking such pointed questions you would have thought we were the kidnappers instead of the victims. I don't think they believed us until Dennis opened his sketchbook. They absolutely gaped at his drawings of the cab driver—the one who met us at Heathrow. Smith left the room and brought back two other agents, who didn't bother to make up creative names for our benefit as they studied the sketches. We had been forgotten.

What surprised me was they seemed more interested in the cab driver than in Mr. Kent. Funny, because if it weren't for Dennis's sketch, I wouldn't have remembered what he looked like. I told the agents he didn't sound British.

They passed the sketchbook back and forth. "Could be Javier. What do you think?"

"Haven't seen his face in years."

Finally, they noticed us staring at them. "We'd like to hang on to this," Jones said, indicating the sketchbook.

I kicked Dennis under the table. We were getting good at non-verbal communication. "Uh, no," he said, "but you can photocopy what you need." Jones left the room with the sketchbook.

Smith made small talk. "You're talented with a pencil, Mr. Ames. You should come work for us." Dennis looked flustered. So did Liza.

Then one of the Mr. No-names told us we should stop worrying and enjoy our holiday; they'd take care of contacting Scotland Yard. He gave Liza his card, which she put away without a glance. I said I'd like a card, too. He chuckled when he handed one over, humoring me, I'm sure. I took a peek before stuffing it into my purse. *Curtis Bland, Central Intelligence Agency.* All right!

"Check that all the pages are there," I whispered when Dennis got back the sketchbook. I had the weirdest feeling about the whole thing. Like we were caught up in something big and were going to be overlooked. They believed our story; they just didn't consider us important in the scheme of things.

"Am I glad we're out of there," I said, once we were back outside. Dennis didn't respond. He had this far-off expression that meant he was memorizing the agents' faces so he could include them in that rogues gallery of a sketchbook he clutched so tightly.

"I don't know what you're talking about," Liza said. "They were most helpful. I'm sure we have nothing to worry about."

She might be right. Maybe Dennis and I had watched too much television. Maybe . . . but I didn't think so. I'd write down the name the agents had mentioned—Hahveeay?—in my journal.

Back at Grosvenor House, Shirl was pacing up and down in our room. She looked lovely in her new turquoise dress, on which she'd pinned the little silver llama Fiona had given her in college. "What took you so long? Fiffy called. We're supposed to meet them in ten minutes."

No time to go into it. "Mostly we waited around," I said, "but they took all our information and photocopied Dennis's sketches."

She went downstairs without me while I changed. I chose a black and white polka-dot sundress, arranged my hair into a French twist, put my feet into new black patent leather sandals. Then I headed downstairs for my first real meal in this country. I looked and felt sophisticated—worthy of Grosvenor House's fancy restaurant.

The MacNeils hadn't arrived, but the Moms and Dennis were waiting. Even Dennis looked respectable. He'd pulled back his hair into a ponytail and had shaved. He wore a blue button-down shirt with short sleeves. So what if he still wore jeans? At least they were clean.

"Sorry we're late, m'dears. Blame the bloody traffic." The MacNeils had arrived.

We were seated in a private dining area, a good idea, for we soon discovered what a character Torquil was. He told one funny story after the other, laughing the hardest at them himself. To say that our party was loud was an understatement. Soon, Shirl, Liza, and Fiona started in on "Do you remembers."

Shirl: Do you remember when you gave me this llama pin?

Liza: Do you remember all the times you were out past curfew? Shirl and I always snuck you back in.

Fiona: Do you remember when Julie got engaged to the gym teacher and announced it at dinner?

For some reason, Shirl did a double take at this. Then there were more memories, and on and on and on. It became apparent, to me at least, that Shirl was asking most of the questions. "I really liked your doctor last night, Fiffy. He reminded me of the one in college. What was his name?"

"Oh, dear, I'm afraid I don't remember."

"Dr. Grace, that's what it was. He was especially nice to you. Don't you remember?"

"That's right. He was kind. I wonder whatever happened to him."

Shirl turned to listen to something Torquil was telling Liza, but I noticed the glint in her eyes and the set of her mouth. Why, she was testing Fiona. She'd set a trap, and Fiona had walked into it. How? And why? What was Shirl up to? Could she really be that upset Fiona had called her Shirley?

Lunch was delicious, and I did justice to every bite. Torquil ordered something called steak tartare. Sickening, raw—I could almost hear it moo. While we were waiting for dessert, I noticed Jeanie's fascination with Dennis. She stared at him until she finally blurted, "What band do you sing with?"

I nearly choked on my water. Jeanie thinks Dennis is a rock star, I thought, howling inside. I gave him a don't-you-dare-disappoint-her kick under the table.

"Uh, I'm between bands right now," he said.

I tuned back in on what Fiona was saying. "We hope you'll be our guests at the theatre tonight."

"Wonderful," Liza almost sang. "I've been dying to see *Miss Saigon*."

Dying. What a choice of words. But honestly, it's playing in Chicago. Why doesn't she see it there?

"Perhaps you can go another night," Torquil said tactfully. "We have tickets for *The Importance of Being Earnest* at the Old Vic."

"Oh, I love that play," I burst out. "We did it in high school last year. My friend Brenda was Lady Bracknell." For some reason, they thought that was funny.

"Then it's settled," Fiona said. "We'll send a car for you."

Torquil took care of the check, and everyone exchanged hugs before saying goodbye.

I followed Shirl back to our room. We were about to have words. I closed the door. "All right, out with it. You're too old to play Nancy Drew."

We engaged in a little game of evasion. "I don't know about that. After all, Nancy Drew was plenty old even when I was a girl."

"Well, not old then," I amended. "But you're not," I grasped for the right word, "subtle."

"I'm just as subtle as you," she returned.

"Yeah, like it's real subtle to faint."

We glared at each other for a full second before bursting out laughing. That's how most of our arguments end. The sight of the other steaming cracks us up every time.

I tried again. "Come on, Shirl. I don't believe you fainted because you were tired. And what was with all the questions at lunch? It was like you were giving Fiona a test."

Shirl turned away from me. She unclasped the silver llama and stared at it, as if it could provide answers. "You're right," she said. "I was testing her."

*J*eanie *knew it was no* use nagging Pops once he'd made up his mind. She would not be going to the theatre.

"Be a waste of good money, our Jeano-Beano. You'd fall asleep before the end of the first act."

"You wouldn't understand it, dear," Mum said. "The humour is really quite sophisticated."

Jeanie didn't care about the play. She wanted to see Dennis and Carly again. She thought Carly might be a fashion model.

Perhaps Mum guessed what she was feeling. "You liked them, didn't you, luv?" Jeanie nodded. "Then I'll tell you a secret. Pops and I are going to invite them to come stay with us in Scotland. Perhaps in a few days, or perhaps they'll join us tonight on the InterCity Sleeper."

"And when I have business in Glasgow, I'll take you all with me, and you can go to a pantomime. Would you like that?" Pops lifted her over his head, and Jeanie giggled and shrieked until he put her down again.

Chapter Eight

"CARLY, BETTER GET UP, DEAR. You'll want a snack before we go the theater."

I awoke instantly, mentally thanking Shirl for rescuing me from one of the dumbest dreams I'd ever had. I was on stage at the Old Vic performing the part of Gwendolyn Fairfax. Dennis played opposite me in the role of Jack/Ernest while his new rock group, "Steak Tartare," sang backup. We took our bows, and the audience cheered. The bright lights didn't prevent me from seeing clearly. Every single person in the audience looked like Fiona—different clothes, but the same face, multiplied by the hundreds.

Shaking my head at the memory, I glanced at my watch and shrieked. "I should have met Dennis hours ago. What will he think?"

Shirl chuckled. "Don't worry about him. He took a nap, too."

"That's good," I said, relieved.

"You're getting along with him better now, aren't you?" She winked at me.

What was she suggesting? "Like I have a choice?"

But Shirl saw right through me and laughed in my face. "Liza and I are going to explore the shops in the lobby. You can meet us there." She looked down at the turquoise dress she still wore. "Will this do for the theater? Or should I change?"

"You look perfect. But maybe a shawl? In case there's air conditioning?"

As soon as Shirl left, I considered my clothes. If there was air conditioning, I'd freeze in a sundress. My brushed-knit, dusty rose pants outfit was a better choice. I undid the French twist and gave my hair a good brushing. I'd wear it down tonight.

I hadn't meant to fall asleep, but I guess I'd needed rest after losing my game of 20 Questions with Shirl. She hadn't budged one inch when I quizzed her about Fiona.

"Something about Fiffy seemed wrong."

"You mean her calling you Shirley?"

"Not just that."

"Then what?" I'd demanded.

Shirl shook her head. "Maybe someday, Carly. It's pretty personal."

Darn. I was determined to find out. While applying my makeup, I thought over Shirl's insinuation. Me and Dennis? No way!

Just before the car came, my stomach felt kind of fluttery. No wonder, really. Why should we trust a strange driver ever again? "Take a good look at the driver," I whispered to Dennis.

"I've already thought of that. And Carly, as soon as I buy a box of pastels, I'm going to draw you in that outfit."

I never know what to do with a compliment, so I blushed.

He laughed. "I'll have to shade your face the same color as your clothes."

Fortunately, the car arrived, putting an end to the embarrassing conversation.

"Finished my business early," a voice boomed. Torquil got out of the car, and Fiona waved from inside. "Thought we'd do the job ourselves," Torquil said. "Thought you might feel more comfortable driving with someone you know." I searched Torquil's face for hidden meaning, but he looked as innocent as a large bald lamb. Just a coincidence, I decided. We all climbed into the car.

Our doubts about Fiona and Torquil were beginning to look ridiculous—they were being so kind to us. As soon as Torquil pulled out, he made the offer. "We're hoping you'll come visit us in Dumfrieshire."

"Wonderful," Liza said.

"Lovely," Fiona added.

Shirl kept quiet, but I thought it was wonderful—and lovely, too. A chance to see Scotland with people who really knew it.

"We're taking the late sleeper from Euston Station tonight," Torquil said. "Will you join us?"

Tonight? Wait a minute. This was happening too fast. Why the rush? What about London?

Shirl must have had the same thoughts. "This is a bit sudden, don't you think? I mean, we just arrived . . ." She sounded confused, and her voice drifted off. After all, Fiona and Torquil didn't know when we really arrived—or did they?

"Bloody inconvenient and all that," Torquil said, "but you see, m'dears, the railway has one of its blasted strikes scheduled. If you don't come tonight, you might not be able to for another week."

"Do come," Fiona urged. "Jeanie has talked about nothing but rock stars and high-fashion models since she met Dennis and Carly."

"Peaceful country, Scotland," Torquil said. "Just what Shirl needs after her illness."

"Please, Shirl, let's do it," Liza said. "We'll see London before we go home."

I wasn't convinced. *We'll do it later* was becoming the theme song of this trip, but it wasn't my decision to make.

"Give us a chance to think about it," Shirl said. "We'll give you an answer as soon as the play is over. Will that be time enough?"

"Right," Torquil agreed. "It will be an easy matter to make reservations."

The rest of the ride was devoted to small talk and admiring London. I wanted to talk to Dennis in private—to tell him about Shirl's reaction to Fiona. And I wanted to ask him what he thought about this new invitation. Why had we been invited to Scotland so suddenly? It was hard to believe these were the same people who'd given us such a cold reception at the university.

The Old Vic was not in the theater district but in a worn-down neighborhood across from Waterloo Station. This was disappointing. What a thrill, though, when we were escorted to our own box. I'd never sat in a box seat before. The few times Shirl and I had seen shows in Chicago, we were seated so high we needed binoculars just to see the stage. The MacNeils must be very wealthy to afford this.

We'd arrived early, a good twenty minutes before the curtain would rise. Dennis and I sat together and looked down at the people in the stalls below. (What we call orchestra or main floor at home.) "Look at all the fur coats, even though it's summer," Dennis said.

I shuddered. "At home they'd be picketed."

Then, from out of the corner of my eye, I noticed Torquil lift his arm. A man in the stalls stood and raised his arm back. Mr. Kent! The same signal he'd given at Limpley Stoke. I looked back at Torquil, but he'd disappeared, and Mr. Kent was making his way out to the lobby.

"Be right back." They looked questioningly at me. "Ladies." I made my exit.

Torquil signaling Mr. Kent. Proof Torquil had something to do with our kidnapping. But why? And what did he want from us now?

I was halfway down the stairs when I saw them standing near the Gents in the lobby. They were quarreling, although I was too far away to hear their words. Torquil handed Mr. Kent some money. Evidently it wasn't enough, for Mr. Kent scowled, and his face reddened. Torquil shrugged before starting back up the stairs. I ducked behind a large potted plant and waited until he passed before risking another peek. Mr. Kent clenched his fist and shook it. Then he returned to the stalls. To see the show? Why bother?

I thought Torquil looked anxious as I took my seat. I ignored him, though, and complained to the others about the long queue in the loo.

Dennis laughed. "Queue in the loo? That's funny."

"We need to talk during intermission," I whispered.

My big chance to see a truly British play at a famous theater in London, and I couldn't concentrate. Dennis seemed to be chuckling in the right places. "Don't you like it?" he whispered.

"It's great," I said, but I could hardly wait until Act 1 was over.

At last the curtain fell, and when the lights came up, I looked down to see if Mr. Kent was still there. He rose, and then I noticed something unbelievable. About five rows behind him, two other men stood together—the cab driver with the odd Spanish name and one of the no-name men from the embassy. Not Curtis Bland, who'd given us his card, but the other guy. Kent started out of the theater with the two men following close behind.

I grabbed Dennis's hand. "Come on."

"We've ordered interval refreshments. Cucumber sandwiches, strawberries and cream, tea, champagne."

"We'll be right back," I promised Fiona, before pulling Dennis out into the hall. I'd figure out some excuse later.

"Carly, what's going on?"

"Mr. Kent. Come on, Dennis." We were going to follow the kidnappers.

*J*eanie *finished her lovely supper* of boiled potatoes and strawberries with clotted cream. Then she and Nanny packed and tidied the hotel room.

"The hotels have maids to do this, Nan," Jeanie objected, but Nanny scrubbed the bathroom sink and refused to listen.

"Nonsense. What will they think of us if we leave things a mess?"

After Nanny declared their surroundings spotless, she settled herself in front of the telly, and Jeanie returned to her book to find out what happened to her favorite Chalet School girl, Joey.

Joey's disappearance turned out to be quite tame. She fell into a deep hole in the ground, which was thrilling enough, but she was rescued too soon. Jeanie was hoping the adventure would last longer, although she was relieved for Joey, of course. What would it be like to disappear? To have Mum and Pops not know where she was at all?

"Nan, would you miss me if I went away?" But Nanny was watching "Coronation Street" and didn't hear.

Chapter Nine

A T FIRST, I THOUGHT WE'D lost Kent and his pursuers among the
hordes of people who were risking the threatening clouds and
darkening sky to gather in front of the Old Vic for a cigarette and a
breath of stale air. But Dennis spotted them and pulled me through
the crowd. We found ourselves in a dark, narrow alley near the theater,
so isolated we felt as if we were miles away.

"Don't they believe in street lights?" I whispered, changing my
mind about the whole venture. "Let's go back before we're caught in
the rain."

Suddenly, maybe twenty feet ahead, we heard a gasp, followed by
groans.

"Shhh," Dennis cautioned. He pushed me into the doorway of an
abandoned storefront, where I crashed against a garbage can. Then he
stepped on something that came to life with a shriek and a hiss. A cat,
I guessed. We couldn't have been more conspicuous if we'd shouted
our presence over a P.A. system.

A light from out of nowhere blinded us. Then we heard racing footsteps in retreat. We were alone with whoever was moaning in agony.

"Someone's hurt," I said.

Dennis rummaged through his pockets. "I still have my lighter." I saw a flicker and a steady light. The flame in the darkness was comforting. I held on to Dennis as we moved toward the sounds. Someone was doubled over between two dumpsters. Dennis held out his light. Mr. Kent—and there was blood everywhere.

Dennis knelt down. "Mr. Kent, it's us. Dennis Ames and Carly Sullivan. We'll get help."

"Too late." Mr. Kent clutched at his stomach.

"Who did this to you?" I said, even though I thought I'd pass out. "Was it Torquil?"

"No," Mr. Kent gasped, grimacing in pain. Then he said something weird. "Send for Loomis." He repeated it. "Send for Loomis." At least, that's what it sounded like.

"Send for who?" But Mr. Kent had nothing more to say. He fell back—lifeless.

"Carly, let's go. Now!"

"We can't just leave him here." My voice was too shrill; I shook all over.

"He's dead, and we know who killed him. The cab driver and that agent. And they might know we know. They flashed their light right in our faces."

He had a point. "Okay, but we'll call the police from the theater."

"No we won't. After the play, we'll use a pay phone far from here. He's dead, Carly. We can't help him."

We heard the first clap of thunder, low and menacing. Numbly, I allowed Dennis to lead me back to the Old Vic. The crowd had dispersed. Only a few stragglers were taking their final puffs.

Fortunately, some part of my brain still functioned. An excuse. We needed an excuse for bolting out and missing Fiona's "interval refreshments." I looked around for inspiration and saw the very thing— a lit cigarette that had been dropped on the steps. Shouldn't be too difficult. I put it into my mouth and sucked in. Foul! I sputtered as I blew the smoke right into Dennis's face.

He jumped back. "What the . . . Carly, what the hell are you doing?"

I repeated the process and blew again. "You've just had a slip, and I was trying to talk you out of it. That's our excuse."

Dennis grabbed the cigarette out of my hand before I could douse him again. "Knock it off!" He threw it on the ground and stomped it out. "Mom won't believe I've quit. What about my car?"

"I'll tell her the truth later. Besides, you've got all summer to quit."

He shook his head. We hurried inside just as the clouds finally burst, and the lights dimmed for the second act.

It worked. Liza and Shirl sniffed; no one asked questions. Okay, I felt guilty. It was a lousy trick to play on Dennis, but I'd had no time to come up with something better. I promised myself I'd mend things between Dennis and his mother as soon as possible.

"Were you smoking?" Shirl whispered in my ear as the curtain rose.

"Of course not," I snapped.

As we settled back in our seats, I glanced at Torquil. I thought he looked relieved. About what? Did Torquil know Mr. Kent was out of everyone's life, especially his own?

The audience gasped as the stage revolved into Cecily's garden. It was a gorgeous set, and I joined the applause, managing to stay focused on the plot for a whole minute before my troubled thoughts took over again.

We'd almost witnessed a horrible bloody murder, and we had discovered a dying—now dead—man. But instead of behaving like good citizens and reporting the crime, we'd fled and were keeping our mouths shut. I didn't agree with Dennis about not going to the police, but I could see his point of view. One of the murderers was an agent, who could certainly kill us off, too, if he saw us as a problem. Our word against a British agent—who would believe us?

I didn't have answers, only feelings. Somehow, we'd stumbled onto something far more serious than our kidnapping, which didn't seem as important now as murder. Who to trust? That was my problem. I remembered what my sophomore English teacher said to me once. "You've got good instincts, Carly. Go with them. They won't let you down."

Okay. Reason said we should contact the authorities immediately. For now, I pushed reason aside. Who did I trust? I trusted Shirl and Dennis and me. Even though I wasn't always sure I liked Liza, she was one of Shirl's oldest friends and Dennis's mother, so she was on the trust list. I did not trust Smith or Jones, who didn't even use their own names, or Javier and the Mr. No-name agent. I reached into my purse and touched Curtis Bland's business card. I'd had good vibes about him but not his associates.

Then I thought about the MacNeils. There was something wrong about Fiona and Torquil, and I was pretty sure they were involved in our kidnapping. Still, Fiona had been Shirl's college friend, and she and her husband had been kind to us. I made up my mind. "Shirl," I whispered, "I think we should go to Scotland tonight."

"You do? What about seeing London?"

"Liza thinks it's okay—that we can come back here before we fly home."

Shirl whispered to Liza, starting a little game of telephone until everyone in our box got the good news.

"Why, Carly?" Dennis whispered.

"I think we'll be safer. Kent said Torquil didn't have anything to do with his murder. We should get out of London."

After curtain call, we walked to Torquil's car. It had stopped raining but was still pretty drippy. I managed to talk to Liza. "Dennis didn't smoke," I said softly. "I asked him to go outside because I needed to stretch. We started talking about London pollution and how the air would be cleaner if we went to Scotland. We lost track of time. The reason we smelled smoky was because we had to go through a crowd of people who were smoking. Dennis hasn't had a cigarette since we left Chicago. Honest."

Liza smiled. "Thank you for telling me, Carly."

I don't know if Liza talked to him. After we returned to the hotel, we didn't have time for anything but a quick pack-up and a difficult explanation to an indignant desk clerk. I didn't blame him; our behavior had been erratic.

Just before we climbed inside the cab that would take us to Euston Station, Dennis pulled me aside. "I called the police. At a phone booth down the street."

"Did you give our names?"

"No, I just said they'd find a dead body in a dark alley near the Old Vic. Then I hung up."

"I hope we won't be sorry," I said, shaking my head.

Liza overheard. "Of course we won't. Just think, Fiffy's home in Scotland. It's a dream come true."

Or a nightmare. I stared glumly out the window all the way to the station.

Later that night, I switched on the little light over my top bunk in our sleeper compartment. Shirl had fallen asleep in the lower one while Dennis and I played Monopoly with Jeanie in the lounge.

I got up to date in my journal, first reading it over from page one. No one would ever believe it. Nothing sounded real. Then I turned to the *Things to Find Out* page and added *Loomis* to my list. Who was Loomis, and why did Mr. Kent want us to send for him?

By chance, my journal opened to the *Things I Want to Do* page. How depressing. The InterCity was taking us far from London, where, truthfully, the pollution hadn't bothered me all that much. Far from London, where all we'd done was go to a drab university building, the embassy, and the theater. And a dark, creepy alley. I didn't want to think about that. I grabbed my pen and added: 4. *Feed the pigeons in Trafalgar Square.*

*J*eanie *snuggled under her covers* in delight. Nanny had actually given her the top berth! "You're becoming more responsible," Nan had said. "I can trust you not to fall down on me."

And it was really late! Because she'd taken such a long nap while Mum and Pops were at the theatre, Pops had let her stay up a whole hour after they'd boarded the train. She'd never stayed up this late before.

Dennis and Carly were great fun. They'd played the London Monopoly game Aunt Jean had given her. It was funny because they didn't know the posh streets from the ones with council housing. Of course, they didn't have time to finish the whole game, but Dennis said they'd play another day and that he was going to win. Jeanie giggled into her pillow. She'd see about that!

She didn't think he was a rock star, after all. He didn't mention music once. Carly said he was a wonderful artist and could draw pictures of her in just a few minutes. Jeanie yawned. She didn't suppose Carly was a model either. She was just frightfully pretty and frightfully nice.

Chapter Ten

H AVE YOU EVER FALLEN IN love with a place at first sight? Like
you knew it was part of you, and you belonged there? That's
what happened to me the minute I saw Scotland. The magic started at
daybreak before we reached Glasgow and transferred from our sleeper
to a commuter train going to Dumfries. I stared out the window, filling
my eyes with green grass, blue skies, rolling hills, purple heather—I
was sure I saw a castle.

Still in a daze, I followed everyone out onto the platform. Fiona
took my hand. "Oh, Carly, you remind me of me the first time I came
here. I didn't think I'd ever want to leave again. But come now, there's
much more to see than the view from the Dumfries railway station."

I followed along to the parking lot, where Torquil's travel van was
waiting. He had called ahead the night before for someone to park it
there. They have three cars—one for town, which is what they call
London, and a van and regular car for home.

"Carly," Liza said, once we were on our way, "did you know
Robert Burns lived the last years of his life in Dumfries?"

"There's a statue on the High Street and a museum and everything," Jeanie added.

"No kidding. You mean we're going to act like tourists and start seeing things?"

"Who was Robert Burns?" Dennis asked.

"Only one of the finest poets who ever lived." Liza gave him one of her honestly-Dennis looks.

"I don't know about that," I said, coming to Dennis's defense, "but I do like most of his stuff. Tell you what, Denny, I'll recite *A Man's a Man for a' that* for you sometime. I memorized it last year for speech team."

He looked surprised but gave me a huge, wonderful smile.

I was surprised, too. When had he become Denny to me? Maybe around the time I started to appreciate that smile. All I knew was I didn't think he was awful anymore. I liked him now—I liked him a lot. And I hated when his mother put him down. Shirl, who knew the poem was about valuing all people, giggled into her fist.

I don't think Liza caught the exchange. She had moved on to discussing golf with Fiona. "Oh, do you play, too? I'd love to . . ."

"Golf is boring," Jeanie said. "Carly and Denny"—so someone had been listening—"will want to do other things—with me."

Everyone laughed and was in great spirits. We had been driving a long time. I checked my watch. Forty minutes had passed since we'd left the station. We'd driven out of town into the country, through a few villages, and were approaching—woods? Not again, I groaned inside.

"I thought you lived right in Dumfries."

Fiona gave her little-bells laugh. "Actually, Dumfrieshire. We've built ourselves a hideaway—a complete break from London."

"It's just around the bend, Carly," Jeanie said. "Right next to the Solway Firth. Wait until you see!"

The van followed the road out of the trees and there, built on a cliff, was the most splendid home I'd ever seen. White adobe bricks, three stories high, curled wrought-iron balconies at practically every window, the house looked like a hacienda. It belonged in Spain, not Scotland.

"So you decided to create a bit of Lima here, Fiona," Liza said.

Fiona smiled. "I've adjusted very well, I think, but sometimes I miss the land of my childhood."

"Oh, hurry and get out," Jeanie said. "We've got horses, Denny. Wait until you see the horses!"

Liza winked at the rest of us. "'Denny,' is it?"

"Our Jeano-Beano was always one for pet names," Torquil said, chuckling.

Jeano-Beano? She wasn't the only one. Dennis and I grinned at each other. But I was pleased. Now I wouldn't have to worry about being teased. Everyone thought Dennis's new nickname was Jeanie's idea.

Fiona showed us to our rooms and told us to come downstairs "for a wee bite" after we settled in.

"Won't we need a map to find our way?" I couldn't resist asking.

Fiona laughed and patted my shoulder. "It's good to have you here, Carly." She dashed away to conquer her next task. I'd decided Fiona was like a little tornado, whirling everyone along into her world.

I looked around at the blue and gold splendor. Each of us had our own room. That made at least four guest bedrooms. We only have two bedrooms in our condo at home, and they're mighty small ones. I opened what I thought was a closet and found—my own private bathroom! I gave my face a thorough scrub, brushed my hair, and went searching for that wee bite.

As one of the MacNeils' "help" cleared the table, Fiona began to make plans. "Jeanie wants you to see the horses," she said, "but that had better keep. They're being exercised now. Perhaps you can help with that chore tomorrow morning."

Some chore. I could hardly wait.

Fiona continued. "Tonight, you're in for a treat. We're going to Dumfries for a ceilidh."

"Kay lee," I repeated. It would be some time before I bumped into its odd spelling. "Ceilidh is Gaelic for a visit," Torquil said. "It's more of a party, actually. A Highlands hoedown—folk songs, dances, and, most important, the pipers."

"And, most important, you'll hear Pops sing," Jeanie corrected him.

"If I'm asked, m'dear."

"Oh, Pops, you'll be asked. You're super."

I was starting to love Jeanie.

She pulled on her mother's arm. "What about now, Mum? What should we do now?"

"I thought a walk to our neighbor might be in order. What do you think?"

Jeanie's eyes sparkled, and she jumped up and down. "Oh, they'll never guess," she breathed. Her enthusiasm was contagious—to almost everyone. But Shirl asked to be excused.

"I'd like to rest, if you don't mind. Oh, I'm all right," she responded to our concerned looks. "But we had such a late night, and I didn't get much sleep on the train."

"Shirl . . ."

"I'm fine, Carly. Let me rest so I'll be ready for the party tonight." She smiled weakly and left the room.

My spirits drooped a little, but Shirl didn't look sick; she looked tired, like she said.

"Moira," Fiona told the girl who had served us, "we'll not need a regular luncheon. Just leave a selection for tea on the sideboard. We'll dine at the Cairndale tonight."

"Very good, ma'am." Moira didn't curtsey, but she might have been thinking one.

"Who do you suppose this mysterious neighbor is?" I whispered to Dennis once we were on our way.

"Probably Mr. Kent's mum," he whispered back.

"Denny, that's awful." But I giggled. What had happened in London seemed unreal and so far away.

We didn't return to the road. Jeanie led us to a wide path through the woods. She danced on ahead with Torquil, Fiona, and Liza, following right behind. Dennis and I brought up the rear.

Soon, we were out of the woods and walking on green rolling turf. A golf course? Liza would be pleased, but I was disappointed. "Your neighbor owns a golf course," I yelled my guess ahead to Jeanie.

"You're wrong, you're wrong, you're wrong," she sang.

And then we saw it. At the base of a green velvet hill sat a perfect ruin of a castle. "Perfect" might be a strange word to describe a ruin, but it was. The castle was shaped like a medieval shield, with a lookout tower on each corner. It even had a drawbridge and was surrounded by a tiny moat.

"Is it real?" Dennis couldn't open his sketchbook fast enough.

"Absolutely," Fiona said. "Welcome to Caerlaverock Castle, built and run by the Maxwell family since 1266, or so people say. The Maxwells are great friends of ours. I'll lend you a pass so you can visit any time you like."

"It looks so small," Liza said. Perhaps she would have preferred a golf course.

Torquil chuckled. "Not at all. Wait until you get closer, m'dear."

I'd had enough chatter. I raced toward the castle, my arms stretched out, attempting to embrace it. A laughing Jeanie danced along beside me.

We dined at the Cairndale Hotel, where the ceilidh was held every Sunday night.

"Aye, the Wallace family does a grand ceilidh." Torquil sounded more Scottish as the hour for the party approached. Normally, he spoke with a regular British accent.

After dinner, we took seats in an elegant ballroom. Then in marched the kilted pipers, their colorful tartans representing many different clans. I'd never cared for bagpipe music, but in the right setting, with people who loved it, the sound was pretty exciting.

Next came the folk dancing. It reminded me of our American square dancing—but much harder. The only things the dancers seemed to move were their feet; the rest of their bodies stayed stiff. Torquil asked me to dance. I shook my head. "I couldn't."

"A fine lassie like yerself? Of course ye'll be dancing. It's not the fling I'm asking ye to do." He showed me a few simple steps, and we joined a set of other couples. I noticed that Fiona was teaching Dennis.

It wasn't long before Denny and I were just another couple having a terrific time. We made mistakes and stepped on toes, but everyone was kind and didn't seem to mind our clumsiness.

Then came the singing. Some of the songs I knew from choir at school—"Coming through the Rye" and "The Bonnie Banks of Loch Lomond," so I sang along. With the others, I joined in the chorus as soon as I figured out the words.

"Torquil," a voice shouted. "Torquil, give us a song." Other voices took up the chant. "Torquil, Torquil. Come on, mon, you've been away too long." Laughing, Torquil consulted with an accordionist and then began to sing in a beautiful tenor voice.

> *Haste ye back, we love you dearly,*
> *Call again ye're welcome here.*
> *May your days be free from sorrow,*
> *And your friends be ever near.*
> *May the path for which you wander*
> *Be to you a joy each day.*
> *Haste ye back, we love you dearly,*
> *Haste ye back on friendship's way.*

Somewhere, toward the middle of the song, I noticed Liza staring at Denny and me. I looked down and saw my hand in his. I don't know how it got there, but it felt right. I smiled at Liza, looked back at Torquil, and left my hand where it was.

Many eyes, including mine, had tears in them when Torquil finished. Then I noticed Shirl. She wasn't just moved by the song, she was sobbing. Tears streamed down her face.

"Shirl needs me." I squeezed Denny's hand before releasing it. "I'll be back." I pushed through the crowd. Shirl was trying to pull herself together by wiping her eyes with a thin tissue. "Are you sick, Shirl? What's wrong?"

She shook her head, murmuring something I had to lean very close to hear. But I couldn't have heard right, for what I thought she said was, "where is Fiona?"

*J*eanie *got up during the night* for a glass of juice and was on her way back to her room when she heard strange noises—like someone crying. They were coming from the guest room Carly's mum was using. The quiet, sad lady was crying again. She wondered why Carly's mother always seemed frightened and unhappy. And why did she always stare at Jeanie in such a puzzled way? Jeanie liked the other guests much better.

Chapter Eleven

W**E SAT ON A BENCH**, Shirl and I, directly across from a horrible stone face sculpted on the castle wall. "Wha daur meddle we' me" were the words chiseled under the mask. Who dares meddle with me? A warning for whoever might threaten its Maxwell lord. Good advice, even for today. Meddling was not a good thing, but I needed some answers; I took the plunge.

"It's time, Shirl. What's bothering you about Fiona?"

Shirl turned to me with tears in her eyes. "Very well," she said, "but give me a few minutes alone to get my thoughts together."

I could wait. I'd been waiting all night. Right after we got home from the ceilidh, Shirl had murmured a quick goodnight and gone straight upstairs. That was the downside to having our own rooms. Before I followed her, I'd whispered to Denny. "I need to get Shirl alone tomorrow morning so she'll tell me what's bothering her."

"Do you think it's about the case?"

I grinned in spite of my worry. I mean—"the case?" Like we were characters in a kids' detective series. "Maybe," I said. Dennis agreed to help. Upstairs, I went into Shirl's room.

She was in her bathroom with the door closed. "Shirl?"

"We'll talk tomorrow, Carly," she called out.

"Okay . . . goodnight then . . ." Tomorrow seemed a long way off.

After breakfast, Dennis offered to go with Jeanie to exercise the horses. "I'll bring my sketchbook and draw a picture of each one. Then you won't miss them so much when you're in London."

Jeanie was so pleased she didn't notice I hadn't volunteered to go along. Fiona and Liza teamed up to play golf, and Torquil announced he had business in his study that would occupy him until noon. Business? What does the man do?

"That leaves Shirl and me." I offered to show her Caerlaverock Castle.

Mrs. Maxwell had waved us through as we approached her small gift shop and café. Not many tourists so far. In fact, we were the only ones. I hoped it would stay that way.

I left Shirl, gathering her thoughts, and entered the great hall. Although much had been done to restore the castle, it was still barren enough to excite my imagination. I'm not interested in castles that are furnished, inhabited, and have tour groups coming through every hour. Where was the wonder in that? I walked into a smaller room. A couple inches lower and I would have grazed my head on the archway. People certainly were shorter in those days. Torquil and Liza had had to duck the day before. I was examining a cubbyhole, wondering if it could be the toilet—how did they manage?—when I looked out the window and saw Shirl beckoning me. Finally!

We met in the great hall and toured silently together. Then she sighed and led me over to a stone bench. "Okay, Carly," she said. "I'll tell you. The problem is Fiona. She isn't Fiona at all. She's an impostor."

I stared at her. "But . . ."

"Oh, I've been through all the 'buts.' She looks like Fiona, aged of course, and she says the right things most of the time. Somehow, she's done the research."

"Look . . ." I began. This was too much! "Are you sure? I mean, people change, and they forget things."

"I'm positive. Believe me, I wish I weren't. I like this new improved Fiona very much."

I decided to play along for the moment. "What was the real Fiona like?"

"Like quicksilver. Like a merry-go-round followed by a roller coaster. She never stopped, and she used people up on her way to nowhere."

"She doesn't sound very nice."

"She wasn't. 'Nice' was never the adjective for Fiffy. She was exciting, flamboyant, fascinating, and people wanted to be around her."

"Including you?"

"Especially me. We were intimate friends. I knew her better than anyone, I think."

"What about Liza?"

"They weren't as close. Besides, Liza was away student teaching in another town, when . . . when it happened."

"When what happened?"

Shirl paused. "It wasn't just girls who couldn't resist Fiona. I saw her go through more boyfriends in a month than I've had in a lifetime. Curfew meant nothing to her. She knew which doors might be neglected and which monitors could be bribed. And she could always count on me to open a window and help her in."

"She couldn't have been a very good student."

"She barely scraped through with Cs, and I'm sure the teachers were just being kind at that because she was from a foreign country. They liked her and made excuses."

I shook my head. "Then how did she get to be a psychologist?"

Shirl gave me a look. Right. The impostor theory. Shirl didn't think the real Fiona was a psychologist. "Getting back to the boyfriends. I tried to talk to her, lots of times, about being careful, but she only laughed at me. 'In my country, we never are near a boy unless we have at least ten long-skirted duennas to frown disapproval at us.' That's what she used to tell me in her pert Spanish accent."

"Spanish?"

"Spanish," Shirl insisted. "Liza thinks it's amusing that Fiona's acquired such a strong British accent in only twenty years."

"Twenty years is a long time. And if Liza doesn't suspect anything . . ."

Shirl snorted. "Liza isn't suspicious of anyone, except her own son."

She had a point. "Go on," I said quietly.

"One day, Fiffy insisted I cut my classes. She said she needed me. I could see how desperate she was, so I agreed. Carly, she was pregnant, and she wasn't sure who the father was."

"Fiona had another child—besides Jeanie?

Shirl glared. "You're not listening. Jeanie's mother is not Fiona. Fiona had no child—ever. What she had was a dirty rotten butcher-job of an abortion!"

"No!"

Shirl's eyes filled again. "It was awful. Fiffy was determined not to go through with the pregnancy. Her family, in fact her whole country, was Roman Catholic, and her father had an important government job. They wouldn't have understood."

"They'd have understood an abortion even less," I said.

"Abortions weren't legal then, of course, but Fiffy had heard of this doctor who'd lost his license because of drunkenness and was willing to perform them—for a price. Fiona always had plenty of money."

"Go on," I said gently. Shirl was having a hard time telling the story. I wondered if she'd ever told anyone before.

"I went with her. No one else knew. His name was Dr. Grace— wasn't that ironic? His office was in his home."

"Dr. Grace. Sounds familiar."

Shirl nodded. "In the hotel restaurant in London. I asked Fiona if she remembered how kind Dr. Grace had been."

That's right. Shirl's test. And Fiona had failed. Suddenly, Shirl let the whole story spill out.

"I stayed in the waiting room with Dr. Grace's wife—a fluffy, silver-haired little thing. Their home was so beautiful I was lulled into thinking everything would be all right. Then I heard Fiffy scream. Just once.

"Soon, Dr. Grace and Fiona came out of the office. They were both kind of stumbling—only he was drunk. Then he just disappeared; he'd already collected his money. Mrs. Grace vanished right after Fiona screamed.

"I helped her outside. She was too weak to take the bus, so I left her sprawled on a sidewalk bench while I hailed a cab. As soon as we reached the dorm, I put her to bed."

Shirl paused, as if to catch her breath. I waited. "That night, she started hemorrhaging and was running a fever. I had to get help, so I knocked on Miss Hazel's door."

"Witch Hazel." I remembered their un-pet name for the dorm mother.

"That's right, only she wasn't witchy that time. She was wonderful. It was the only time in four years I saw her act human. She got Fiona to the infirmary and called a doctor, Dr. Arnold. Then she made us tell her the whole story, and she promised not to tell anyone. She never did."

"Did you report Dr. Grace?"

Shirl shook her head. "No, we were afraid we'd be in legal trouble, too." This I could understand, considering all that had happened to Denny and me lately. "Dr. Arnold stopped the bleeding and put Fiona on antibiotics. She stayed in the infirmary for a few days. Miss Hazel and I told everyone she had the flu, so they wouldn't try to visit her. When Fiffy felt better, she went to see Dr. Arnold. He told her she could never have children."

"Because Dr. Grace botched the abortion?"

Shirl nodded.

"That's awful."

We sat silent, thinking. Shirl's story explained a lot, like her behavior, but it opened the door to new puzzling questions. No wonder Shirl had fainted when Jeanie introduced herself.

"Could Jeanie be adopted?" I asked, already knowing the answer.

"And look so much like her mother? I don't think so, do you?"

Slowly, I shook my head. "Couldn't she have had surgery? Or maybe Dr. Arnold was wrong."

"I thought of that, but too many things don't add up: calling me Shirley, saying that Dr. Grace was kind, so many little things. Remember, I knew Fiona well. No, Jeanie's mother is not Fiona Douglas."

"Then who is she, and why did we even come here?"

"Will ye be wanting to stay much longer?" a voice interrupted us. Startled, we turned around. It was pleasant Mrs. Maxwell, looking anxious. "I need to drive into Dumfries for some shopping," she explained, "and as ye be the only visitors, I was wondering how much more time ye'll need."

"Oh, we can leave now, Mrs. Maxwell," Shirl said. "We lost track of time."

"Aye, that can happen in such a place."

I had an idea. "Mrs. Maxwell, could we go with you? My mother and I would love to see the Robert Burns home. We could call the MacNeils and tell them we won't be back for tea."

Mrs. Maxwell smiled. "Lovely, lovely. My errands should take several hours. Aye, ye'll be grand company."

Perfect. Neither Shirl nor I were ready to face the MacNeils, and we still needed to decide what to do. Shirl nodded and looked relieved.

I made the phone call from Mrs. Maxwell's kitchen. Oddly, Dennis answered. "Denny, why did you answer? What's up?"

"Turmoil, commotion, pandemonium, that's what. Torquil just left. Seems a private investigator he uses sometimes has been murdered in London. The police want to talk with him. Torquil's headed there now. And get this, the murdered man's name was Kent Travis."

Mr. Kent—a private eye? I felt sick.

*J*eanie spread all of Denny's sketches across her bed. Which ones should she ask Mum to have framed? She loved them all, especially the one of her on Trouble's back. Trouble belonged to Pops, and she wasn't allowed to actually ride him, but her friends in London wouldn't know that.

Speaking of trouble, she'd rather not go downstairs for a while. Such a fuss over that awful Mr. Travis. Well, he was awful before he was dead, but nicer than his creepy driver—that dark fellow who spoke with a Spanish accent. Jeanie wondered why he had been hanging around the stables. It felt like he was watching her. No, he was probably only looking for Pops.

Chapter Twelve

TWO DAYS WENT BY, AND still we waited for Torquil to return from London. The murder had unnerved everyone, no matter how much they knew. Shirl and I had come to an uneasy agreement. We would stay a little longer and try to figure out what was happening. "Even if she's not the right Fiona, I think the MacNeils are okay," I'd told Shirl.

"Well, I think they paid someone to kidnap us, so we wouldn't find out she's an impostor."

"That doesn't necessarily make them dangerous."

"And you call me naïve. Wake up, Carly. Torquil is in London because of a murder. They have friends who get murdered. I don't know anyone who's been murdered, do you?"

I'd wanted to say, "Yes, and so do you," but kept still. Better for Shirl not to learn that Mr. Travis and Mr. Kent were the same person and that her daughter had heard the murdered victim's dying words. I mean, if she was so freaked out by a long ago abortion, how would she react? But I had to say something. "He wasn't Torquil's friend; he was a business associate."

"Monkey business, if you ask me." Shirl seemed determined to have the last word, but she did try harder and started acting less stressed-out around Fiona.

Several days later, while the three so-called friends, Fiona, Shirl, and Liza, went to high tea at Threave Gardens and Nanny took Jeanie to "the pictures," Denny and I walked over to Caerlaverock Castle. Mrs. Maxwell waved us through. Then she called out a cheery invitation. "Come back for a spot of tea and fresh oatcakes before ye leave, dearies."

"You bet, Mrs. Maxwell," Dennis shouted back.

We walked around the grounds holding hands, the first time since the ceilidh. "Do you realize we met one week ago today?" I said.

"Like an anniversary?" He grinned at me.

I blushed and couldn't think of another thing to say.

We climbed to the top of a manicured, lime-green hill, where we sat and gazed at the peaceful Solway Firth. Dennis and I needed to pool everything we knew. I started first with Shirl's story about the abortion and also about seeing Torquil and Kent together at the Old Vic.

Denny looked sad. "I hope you're wrong. The MacNeils have been great to us. Fiona said she'd check into the art programs at Edinburgh University. Maybe I could come back and study someday." He paused. "She taught me that folk dance, too . . ."

Great. Dennis had a crush on Fiona. I knew she was gorgeous, but she was old, for heaven's sake.

". . . and if she hadn't taught me how to dance, I couldn't have danced with you." He squeezed my hand.

Flustered, I took my hand back. So maybe he didn't have a crush. "I . . . I like them, too, but something is going on. Haven't you noticed anything? What does Liza say?"

"To me? You've got to be kidding."

Dennis promised to keep his eyes and ears open. He even said he'd try to have a conversation with his mother. Oh, wow.

Mrs. Maxwell yoo-hooed us, and we joined her for tea. I took a bite of an oatcake, which tasted like sawdust, but went overboard on homemade scones, covered with clotted cream.

That afternoon, using my journal for reference, I listed everything I knew about Fiona. I divided it into two parts: Fiona in the 70s and Fiona in the 90s. I was looking for clues, anything that might give a hint to Fiona MacNeil's identity—if she was an impostor. One thing jumped out. Nanny! Nanny, who'd turned out to be the colorless Miss Grainger we'd met back in London, told us that no one had called Fiona "Fiffy" since she'd been a little girl. How long had they known each other?

Nanny and Jeanie hadn't returned from the movies, so I went in search of Moira, who enjoyed a good chat. I found the maid of many duties in the parlor. She smiled at me and put down her duster. "Hi, Moira, I was wondering something. How long has Nanny been with Mrs. MacNeil?"

"Why, all her life, miss. Nanny has watched over Mrs. M. since she was a wee one in Peru. And now she's Mrs. M.'s secretary, when she's not taking care of young Jeanie."

All her life! "Wow," I said, because I had to say something, "that's dedication." It was hard for me to imagine proper Nanny lying, but you never knew . . .

The Moms and Fiona returned from Threave Gardens. Shirl and Liza went to their rooms to write letters. I learned that Fiona was resting in the garden, so I poured two cups of tea, adding cream and sugar to Fiona's. Carly the Sleuth, on the job. "May I join you?" I asked, handing her a cup, even though I knew she'd just had tea.

"Please do." She accepted the tea and patted the lawn chair next to her. "You've come at a difficult time, Carly. I hope it hasn't been too stressful for you."

She had no idea, but I shook my head. "I wondered—did you know the man who was murdered?"

"No, but such an awful thing, murder. I've known of so many."

An opening. "You mean when you lived in Peru?"

"Yes, although . . . Oh, I don't suppose you would be interested."

"Oh, I would!" I sounded too eager. "I mean, Shirl never told me why you lived there."

"It's not an unusual story. Many people from the U.K. lived in Peru. My father worked at the copper mines. He had attended university in your country, where his great friend was Peruvian. After graduation, both of them went to Lima and became quite successful. Father met Mother at a dance. Her father had come from Liverpool to work on the railway. They fell in love, were married, and I came along." She grew quiet as if she were lost in memories.

"Were you happy?"

Fiona smiled. Sadly, I thought. "I had a lovely childhood. My mother and I were close, and although I rarely saw my father, we had jolly times together when I did. I learned to speak Spanish, as well as English, though most of my friends were British. I was a privileged child—parties, good schools, music and dancing lessons. Oh, it was lovely . . ."

Her voice faded off. I was getting nowhere. "Shirl told me your father worked for the government?"

"He did, later, especially after Mother died. But for father, mining came first."

"Then you went to college," I said, and waited expectantly. I thought Fiona looked uncomfortable, but it might have been my imagination. She never had the chance to respond, for Jeanie burst into the garden.

"I'm home," she announced.

"We see that, dearie," Fiona said. "How were the pictures?"

"Lovely." Jeanie dismissed her afternoon. "Denny and I need Carly. Right now. We're going to walk along the shore."

"You're not giving Carly a choice," Fiona scolded.

But I thought she looked relieved. "That's okay," I said. I hadn't learned anything useful—this time.

We were walking along the Solway Firth, hunting for the odd blue and gray shells you find in the sand, when I blundered upon one of our biggest discoveries yet.

"Jeanie, when we go back, could we look at photo albums? You know, of you and your family, your mom in Peru and at college. That sort of thing."

Although I had ulterior motives for asking, I was unprepared for Jeanie's reaction. She turned pale and shook her head violently. "They're all gone," she said, her voice trembling. "Stolen."

Denny and I listened with our mouths open while Jeanie told us the MacNeils' house had been burglarized. "February last," Jeanie said.

Fiona's jewelry, a small amount of money, some business journals, and all her photo albums had been taken. I let Dennis take charge while I digested this information. "Was anybody hurt?" he asked.

"No one was home," Jeanie said shortly.

"I'll bet the police swarmed the place."

Jeanie looked surprised. "No, they didn't. Pops didn't call the police. He called a detective agency. That's when he met Mr. Travis. Mr. Travis tried to find Mum's things, but he never did . . ." Her voice faded in confusion.

So that's how Kent entered the picture.

"You didn't like him, did you?" I asked gently. "Kent Travis, I mean."

"No!" Jeanie shouted. She ran farther up the beach, right next to the water, where she began digging holes in the wet sand.

"Go and ask her why," Dennis insisted.

I shook my head. "No, I can't pump a ten-year-old kid about her parents. It's not fair."

"I guess you're right," he said.

It was hard not to probe, though, when Jeanie probably knew plenty. Once again, I was grateful I'd made my double-Fiona list because something else popped into my mind. "Denny, I remember something. In college, Fiona never had her picture taken. Shirl has photos of all her other friends, but not her. I always thought that was so cool because I don't like having my picture taken either. But now, I don't know . . ."

Dennis nodded. "Add that to the missing photo albums, and it's like Fiona's past is being erased."

"February. The same month we got our invitations to Fiona's lecture. Could be a coincidence. I thought maybe some secretary sent them to us by mistake. Now, I'm not so sure . . ."

Dennis frowned, and his eyebrows almost met in the middle. He stayed silent for so long, I offered him a pound for his thoughts.

"They're worth at least that," he said, coming out of his trance and grinning. "I was thinking we need to find ourselves a good-sized library."

"What for?"

"Research. What was going on in Peru in the mid-70s—what's going on there now. I don't know anything about Peru, do you?"

Visions of llamas climbing Machu Picchu came into my head. Tourist stuff. I shook my head. "You may be right," I said. "We need a library."

A subdued Jeanie joined us. Silently, we started back to the house. She came to life, though, when we turned up the drive and saw the van parked out front. "Oh good, Pops is home."

She rushed into the house but was thwarted by Nanny, who insisted Jeanie wash up immediately for "din-din."

Denny and I found Torquil in the lounge, sipping a drink. "I'm sorry about your friend." I felt uncomfortable pretending we knew less than we did.

Torquil seemed tired but smiled at us. "Thank you, Carly. He wasn't my friend, actually. I doubt if he had any friends. The only one who'll miss Travis is his mother." So Mum wasn't dead.

"Are you finished with your business in London?" Dennis asked.

"Yes, for the moment, but I should pop up to Glasgow tomorrow. I was thinking the two of you, and Jeanie, might like to go with me. My sister and her children live there, and Jeanie loves to spend time with them."

"That would be great," Dennis said. All we had to do now was convince Torquil to make a slight change in plans—to take Jeanie to her aunt's and us to the Glasgow library.

*J*eanie *pushed the potato around* her plate, too excited to eat. What fun she would have in Glasgow! She loved Aunt Jean; why, she was named after her. And Bunny and Angie weren't just cousins; they were great friends. They'd make each other laugh all day long, even without the pantomime. Carly and Denny were old. They'd probably rather do something else. Good. She didn't want to talk about the robbery, not ever again. It had changed Mum and Pops. It had changed everything!

Chapter Thirteen

IT ALL FELL INTO PLACE on the road to Glasgow. I'd expected resistance from Jeanie, but for some reason we'd become low items on her top ten list. All she talked about was seeing her cousins, and she cared little about our wishes.

"We'll ride bikes and play darts and go to the pantomime. We always have such fun." She sighed in ecstasy.

"Sounds great for you, Jeanie," Dennis said, taking charge, "but I was thinking maybe Carly and I could go to the library, instead."

"Library? Why?" Torquil asked from the driver's seat, where he was concentrating on the sudden start to city traffic. Jeanie sat up front with him while Denny and I occupied the rear.

"I'd like to find out about art schools in Scotland," Dennis explained.

I hopped in with a bigger lie. "And I'd like to look up information about tartans. You know, get a head start on a research paper for school."

"What do you think, Torquil?" Dennis persisted.

Torquil switched mental gears easily. "Aye, you'll find a grand library near my sister's place. I'll drop you off there."

Fine. We smiled our thanks at him.

Jeanie looked disgusted at our preferring libraries to bikes, darts, and pantomimes. We had taken a flying leap off her top ten chart, landing at about 37—if that.

"Tell us about Glasgow." I wanted to change the subject now that things were settled. "I've heard it's got a lot of slums."

"Well, it used to," Torquil conceded, "but they've done a grand job of cleaning it up. Beautiful city now. Beautiful Victorian city on the bonnie banks of the River Clyde."

Simultaneously, Jeanie and Torquil burst into song:

> *Roamin' in the gloamin'*
> *on the bonnie banks of Clyde.*
> *Roamin' in the gloamin'*
> *with my lassie by my side.*
> *When the sun has gone to rest,*
> *that's the time that we love best.*
> *Oh, it's lovely roamin' in the gloamin'.*

"That's the song the cab driver sang in Bath," I interrupted, without thinking.

Torquil turned sharply and stared at me. Our car slowed down, and a car that had been following too close behind squealed its brakes and veered sharply into the next lane, barely missing us.

"Blithering idiot, so bloody close. Are ye tryin' to get us all killed?" Torquil yelled, turning his attention back to the road.

Really, it was both drivers' fault, and we were "bloody" lucky not to have been hurt. I looked over at the other car. The driver gave us the finger but turned his face away quickly when our eyes met. Javier! Following us? A coincidence? Seeing me had flustered him, or was he flustered because I'd seen him? And what was wrong with Jeanie? She was staring after the car, and her face had turned white, drained of everything but her reddish-brown freckles.

Finally, we settled down, except for Torquil, who still shook as he kept his eyes on the road. At least my slip had been forgotten. Torquil wasn't supposed to know we'd been in Bath. Of course he did know—if he'd arranged for the kidnapping, but we were supposed to pretend he didn't. The whole thing was ridiculous—these unspoken rules for a dangerous, confusing game. I'd be glad when it was over—whatever it was.

"Welcome to Glasgow," Torquil announced, pointing to the sign.

I was surprised by the beauty of the city—impressive tall buildings, lovely green parks. I'd heard stories of slums, gangs, and drugs. Probably true, but not the whole picture. Like people visiting Chicago and expecting to see clones of Al Capone.

Torquil pulled in front of a great library and pointed out our location on the small map he gave Denny. "Here we are on North Street, and here's my sister's place." He marked both spots with an X and wrote down a phone number. "If you finish early, give Jean a ring. Otherwise, I'll return for you here at five. Will you be getting hungry?"

We shook our heads, having eaten a large brunch. We wished Jeanie, who thought we were deranged, a lovely day. Torquil drove off, and we confronted Glasgow's massive 19th century Mitchell Library. Armed with Dennis's sketchbook and my journal, we were ready for work.

Denny, who came from a small town in Wisconsin, looked overwhelmed by the Mitchell's size. "Wasn't coming to a large library your idea?" I teased, realizing it was no problem. A Chicago-born person like me knows how to conquer a strange, immense library. Ask for help.

Soon, we were seated at two ends of a long table. Dennis had a stack of thick books to wade through. For now, I was content with the "P" volume of an encyclopedia. I planned to get a quick historical overview and then browse through microfilm of old newspaper articles.

What struck me immediately was the violence of Peru's history. It seemed to have been founded by greed. And I thought the Spanish Inquisition, which held Peru in its grasp for years, seemed almost pleasant compared to what came after. Revolution, terrorism, stark poverty, military overthrow—that was Peru's story. I tried to place the gentle woman we called Fiona in such a setting but failed. She didn't fit.

I remembered Fiona telling me her father worked for the Peruvian government. Which government? I checked the encyclopedia for dates. From the late sixties to the mid-seventies, a military junta had taken charge, and its leader was a General Juan Velasco. Fiona's father worked for him? Velasco didn't sound exactly pro-British—certainly not pro-U.S. I shuddered at some of his hateful remarks about my country. Strange, Velasco was replaced in 1975, the year Fiona graduated and returned to Peru. And Shirl and Liza never knew anything about her again—until Shirl picked up a magazine in a dentist's office in Chicago.

I browsed through an excerpt from Peru's constitution that looked similar to ours—on paper, that is. I read on and on. What a terrifying place to live. And I'd only read a watered-down encyclopedia account. I looked across at Dennis, who seemed both engrossed and disturbed by what he was reading. Time for the newspaper articles. I went in search of the friendly librarian, who'd started us on our quest.

After a while, the articles seemed the same—kidnap, torture, murder. One terrorist group's practice was to hang dead dogs as a warning to inhabitants who failed to follow "The Way." The government was almost as vicious. I read an account of a man who was the only survivor of a terrorist attack. The government then had him killed because they figured he must have been guilty of something if the terrorists had allowed him to live. After reading about Peruvian prisons, I decided I'd rather die than spend even one day there. It was interesting in an insane way, but I found nothing to explain why anyone would switch places with Fiona Douglas.

One more try. I called up an article that had a fascinating title: "Shining Path Resumes Terrorism." Shining Path—a terrific name! A name to stir up the imagination! I had become numb to the violence. Let's see—a terrorist group, squashed after its leaders were captured several years ago, was making a comeback. Bombing and assaults were on the rise again. The article speculated that one leader, Javier Estaban, who'd disappeared at the time of the arrests, might not be dead after all.

Javier? A common name, surely, but I flashbacked to the U.S. Embassy and recalled the agent's words as he examined Denny's sketches. "Javier. I haven't seen his face in years."

Eagerly, I read on. The Shining Path, known also by its Spanish name, "Sendero Luminoso," had acknowledged responsibility for recent attacks causing the deaths of over four hundred people.

Sendero Luminoso, I wrote. *The Shining Path.* Sendero Luminoso. Why did that sound familiar? Had I heard those words before? I sat very still, chewing the eraser off my pencil, and allowed my mind to wander back over the last ten days until it focused on a dark alley near an old theater, where I had asked a dying man, "Who did this to you?" And the man answered, "Send for Loomis."

"That's it," I whispered. He didn't ask us to send for Loomis; he answered my question. He said, "Sendero Luminoso." The Shining Path murdered Kent Travis. I remembered our near miss with Javier a few hours before, and I looked around for Denny. I had to tell him right away.

But when I returned to our table, Dennis had vanished. At least, that's how it seemed. I almost expected to see dead dogs hanging from his chair and was so scared that if agent Curtis Bland had come along, I would have thrown myself into his arms.

"Carly, wait until you see what I've got!"

Dennis. I almost passed out in relief. "Where were you?"

"Photocopy machine. What's wrong? You look sick. Oh, never mind. Look at this first." He plunked down an open book in front of me.

"So?" I was sure I had bigger news.

"So everything. Look at the photograph. Look carefully!"

A black and white photo of General Velasco and his family, taken in 1970. I studied the faces—and stopped cold. The general, his wife, two sons, a daughter. Fiona! No doubt about it. Petite. Dark curly hair, though it was long then, and sparkling fun eyes. Something about the mouth and eyes seemed different, but it was she. I read the caption. "Nineteen-year-old daughter, Benita."

Why was Benita Velasco pretending to be Fiona Douglas MacNeil? And what had happened to the real Fiona?

*J*eanie sat in the small, darkened auditorium with Bunny and Angie. So far, it had been a lovely pantomime about Jack and a golden goose. Aunt Jean would return when the performance ended and take them to a restaurant for tea.

"Excuse me, miss. Be ye Jeanie MacNeil?"

"Yes," Jeanie said to the kind-looking man who tapped her on the shoulder.

"There be two waiting for ye in the foyer. Americans, likely, by the sound of them."

Oh, bother. Jeanie didn't want to miss one minute of the program. "What do they look like?"

"The girl has lovely long blonde hair. And the boy has long hair, too, though not lovely."

Jeanie nodded. "Carly and Denny. I knew they'd get tired of the library. Go get them, please."

The man shook his head. "No, miss. They were quite insistent ye should go to them."

Jeanie whispered to Angie, then went into the foyer. She spotted Carly looking out the doorway. "Come on, Carly," she called, "we're missing the pantomime."

Carly didn't seem to hear; she didn't even turn around, so Jeanie went up to her.

"Carly . . ."

The girl turned around.

"You're not . . ." But that was all Jeanie was permitted to say.

Chapter Fourteen

"SENDERO LUMINOSO? HOLY SHIT!"

Several people walking by stared their disapproval.

Dennis lowered his voice. "Carly, you don't think we were kidnapped by the Shining Path?"

It was past five o'clock. We had photocopied everything we thought important and were becoming impatient waiting outside the library for Torquil.

"They must be the kidnappers. Think about it." I began to itemize, using my fingers as props. "One: that CIA agent, Curtis Bland, identified the cab driver as Javier. Two: the newspaper article said a man named Javier might have escaped when the top Senderistos were captured. Three: I saw Javier and an agent, if he really was one, leaving the Old Vic and following Kent. And four: Kent accused the Sendero Luminoso of stabbing him. It all adds up," I concluded.

"And equals what?" Dennis asked irritably. I think he was hungry. "Look, Carly, I read more than just the encyclopedia and a few newspaper articles. The Shining Path kidnaps people, all right, before slitting their throats and gouging out their eyeballs. They don't provide beds, picnic breakfasts, and then ring for a cab so their victims can escape."

It did sound ridiculous. "Maybe Javier doesn't want anyone to know he's alive. Maybe he really was working for Kent Travis."

"That's possible, I guess," Dennis admitted. "Maybe Kent stumbled on to the truth about Javier and had to be eliminated."

Eliminated? Like on a TV show? Were we really having this conversation?

I had a thought. "If it weren't for your sketch, I wonder if Javier's identity would still be a secret."

Denny looked pleased. "It did shake them up."

And there was our near miss of a car accident. Forget coincidences. There were no coincidences in this strange plot. Javier had followed us to Glasgow.

My stomach rumbled from hunger—and fear. What was keeping Torquil? I looked at my watch. 5:30. I suggested we call Jean, and Denny pulled out the map where Torquil had written the phone number. "I'll call from a library pay phone," he said. "You wait here for Torquil. He's probably stuck in traffic."

So I sat on a bench and waited some more. I'd wanted to make the call, just to be doing something, just to have a break from my awful thoughts. The worst being: what if Torquil and Fiona—no, Benita— were involved with the Shining Path? I had to start calling her Benita, at least in my head, but it was hard. The name didn't suit as Fiona did. I wished the Moms had come with us. Had we left them in the clutches of one of the worst terrorist groups in the world?

As soon as I saw Dennis coming down the library steps, I knew something had happened. I rushed to meet him. "What's wrong? Wasn't Jean home?"

"No, the phone kept on ringing. But never mind that. The newspapers were just delivered. I swiped this one. Look!"

His hand shook as he held out a copy of the Glasgow Herald. *Wanted for Questioning in London Murder: Police Search for Two American Teens*. It wasn't the main article, but it was still on the front page. And underneath was a sketch of the teens—us! It was a sketch Dennis had drawn, probably photocopied at the U.S. Embassy before Kent was killed. What was going on?

We looked at each other in horror. Here we stood—living advertisements for the newspaper, ready to be picked up by both the good guys and the bad, without being able to tell the difference.

"Let's get out of here!" I said.

We wandered aimlessly, trying to avoid people heading home from work, many carrying newspapers. We ducked behind posts and into phone booths and doorways. Our efforts not to look conspicuous only made us more so. As we passed a park, I noticed a clump of bushes and pulled Dennis into them. "We're wasting time," I said. "We need a plan."

We collapsed on the ground, emotionally exhausted. "You first," Dennis said. "Hunger and fear have done bad things to my brain cells."

"Well, I don't think Torquil is coming back. Either he never intended to or something's happened."

Denny nodded, perhaps trying to get his brain cells functioning again. "I agree. I didn't notice before, but it seems funny now—Torquil giving us just his sister's phone number. No address and no business or mobile numbers."

"Let me see the map," I said.

We examined it—just an X placed on the street where his sister lived.

"We're near there," Denny said. "Why don't we walk down the street. Maybe we'll see Torquil's car."

A good idea, but . . . I looked at Denny's long hair and Iron Maiden tee shirt. "You're too conspicuous. Someone will notice you."

Dennis hooted. "I'm conspicuous? What about you, Goldilocks?"

True. No two people could be more mismatched or obvious. "I'd still attract less attention. But okay, I'll just find a pay phone and call Jean's house again. You stay here."

Dennis didn't like it, but he agreed to remain hidden. Maybe he figured that someone would remember having seen the foul-mouthed American at the library when they looked at their newspaper. He found a rubberband in his jeans pocket. "Pull your hair back. At least it will look different from the sketch."

I did better than that. I took a large barrette from my purse and gathered my hair into a twist at the base of my neck. "Hurry back," Dennis urged. He said it lightly, but I could read the look in his eyes.

"Don't worry," I said, although I was scared stiff. I returned to a phone booth where we had concealed ourselves a short time before and called Jean's house. I let it ring ten times before I finally hung up.

Now what? I'll admit it—I wanted my mother. Was Dumfries long distance? Did they still call it a "trunk call," like in old British movies? And how did you reverse the charges? To my relief, I had enough coins to fill the operator's demands and soon heard the phone ring.

"MacNeils," a familiar voice said. Nanny!

"Oh, Miss Grainger, I'm glad you're home. This is Carly Sullivan."

"Oh . . . yes?" Her voice sounded uncertain, and I could hear other voices in the background. "Wait a minute, please."

"It's them," I heard Nanny stage-whisper.

"Keep them on the line," a strange man whispered back.

I hung up.

I'll bet I could list the few times in my life I've cried. This was one of them. The tears poured, and I could barely control the sound effects that went with them. I didn't think about being noticed as I walked blindly back to the park. My anguish wasn't caused just by fear, although I was plenty frightened—for us and for the Moms. But it was getting cold, too, and I was hungry, and I had to go to the bathroom.

I stopped at a public W.C. near the park and took care of one of the problems. I also finished my cry and washed my face, drying it the best I could with a rough paper towel. Denny must not see me looking so desperate.

He looked pretty desperate himself by the time I finally joined him. "Where were you? You've been gone half an hour! I was going nuts trying to decide if the cops or Javier had nailed you."

I explained about the phone calls. "Then I had to find a bathroom," I added.

"I resent that," Dennis said, but he sounded less angry. The attempts to conceal my tears hadn't succeeded. "While you were enjoying modern conveniences, I had to make do with these bushes."

"Gross." I giggled. It felt less scary not being alone. "So what should we do next?"

"Eat. I can't think beyond that. We'll need to be careful, though. We don't want to be recognized."

We walked toward George Square, closer to the shopping districts. Everywhere, there were posters advertising a jumble sale at St. Andrew's Parish. The very thing! Plain, worn clothes would make a great disguise—if only St. Andrew's weren't far away. Another answer was right next to us—a barbershop, still open. "You or me?" Dennis asked.

"You, I think. I'm not sure if girls in Scotland get their hair cut in barbershops. Besides, my hair is less noticeable now."

"You win, unfortunately," Dennis said.

"Do you have enough money?"

"For a haircut. Not much more."

Thanks to my trusting parent, I had a lot. But how long would it have to last? I blinked. Shirl. Here's hoping she still trusted me.

Dennis noticed a basic fast food place down the street. "We'll meet there in an hour."

I put my vegetarian impulses on hold; I could taste that burger already. But it would be safer if we weren't seen together until we looked different. First opportunity, I'd cut my hair, too. "While you're at the barber's, I'll try to find that jumble sale."

Dennis agreed, although he cautioned me not to stray too far. "One hour, that's all, and if something goes wrong, call the police."

"You got it. Safety first, even if it means jail." Before I left, I touched on my greatest fear. "While you're saying goodbye to your greasy locks, try to figure out how we can contact Shirl and Liza."

"Count on it. Take care, Carly."

"*P*lease," *Jeanie whimpered, "please let* me go. I'll find my own way home. You won't even have to bother."

The woman reached over to the back seat and slapped Jeanie hard across the face. "Sit still," she hissed, "or something worse than a slap will happen."

Jeanie lay down and drew her knees up to her chest. She held her hands in front of her face, trying to keep her pain and fear private.

The couple had stopped looking like Carly and Denny almost immediately. A few blocks from the theatre, they drove into an alley and pulled off their blonde and black wigs. They stuffed them into tote bags and then put on jumpers, hiding their American-looking shirts. "Out," they'd insisted, and forced Jeanie into another car.

She'd have to help herself. Bunny and Angie would tell their mother she'd gone with Carly and Denny. Pops wouldn't even guess something was wrong until after he picked them up at the library at 5:00.

The man and woman were talking in the front seat. Jeanie strained to listen. They were speaking Spanish very fast. Mum had taught her some Spanish, but she always spoke slowly and clearly for Jeanie.

"Velasco." That was a word she knew, sort of. Mum had talked about someone named Velasco in Peru, but Jeanie had thought it boring and hadn't paid much attention.

"Diamante."

Diamante? Could that mean diamond? She wished they would slow down.

Then they started quarreling. Something about el aeroplano. They were talking about leaving in an airplane. But the woman didn't want to go until they were paid—dinero, money.

But if they left in an airplane, what about her? Would they take her with them?

Chapter Fifteen

ON THE 9:30 TRAIN TO Edinburgh, a handsome young man sat in an aisle seat. His short dark hair curled slightly. He wore a navy blue polo shirt under a comfortable looking gray fleece jacket. The worn backpack in his lap must have been important, for he clenched it tightly as he tried to sleep. But the jostling of the train, or perhaps his own thoughts, kept jarring him awake.

A few rows back, on the opposite side but also on the aisle, sat a girl, trying not to notice the young man. The color and style of her hair and clothes were a mystery, for she wore a knitted wool cap pulled down past her ears, and she'd wrapped herself in a stadium blanket of Black-Watch plaid.

Who were those attractive, interesting people? Why, Denny and me, of course. Oddly enough, the jumble sale had been responsible for this late-night trip to Edinburgh.

All things considered, I had had the best time. I bought plain-colored polo and tee shirts, hoodies, caps, the comfy blanket, and backpacks for both of us. And all for fifteen pounds. I changed in the church restroom and was about to leave, when I decided to check out the sale once more to see if I could buy some underwear, for me at least.

A woman, maybe about sixty, was elbowing others out as she sorted through second-hand baby clothes, forming stacks of what appeared to be "take" and "reject" piles. Another woman, grinning mischievously, tapped her on the shoulder. "Och, Betty, is there an announcement ye need to be makin'?" Considering Betty's age, I'd been wondering the same thing, so I kept on listening.

"Mary MacLeod, ye startled me. I'm buying these for my Flora's wee one, just born today."

"Nae! And I didna even know yer Flora was married."

"Aye, she married a crofter. He's a grand mon, but it's a hard life they're havin' at the back o' beyond." Betty told Mary, while I eavesdropped shamelessly, that Flora needed help with the newborn and the other "bairns."

"I'll take the 21:30 from Queen Street Station to Edinburgh this night, and then transfer to the Kyle line for Isle of Skye."

"Ye're a fine mother, Betty. Blessings on ye all."

I'd heard enough. It was getting late, so I hurried to the restaurant before Dennis decided to call the police. But he wasn't there. I tried to remain calm—just stood and weighed my options while looking around the restaurant.

"Who you looking for, Carly?"

I jumped in fright until—"Denny! Denny, you look terrific!" If it weren't for his voice and shirt, I wouldn't have recognized him at all.

He gave a pathetic version of a smile. "Thanks, but I feel bald."

I told him what I'd overheard at the jumble sale, and he caught on fast.

"Trains. I like that idea. No one pays much attention to anyone else on trains. We should get out of Glasgow, and the Isle of Skye sounds remote enough. We should be safe for a while."

Dennis changed into his new old clothes, and we purchased "take away" burgers, chips, and Cokes. We made three important stops on the way to Queen Street Station. At an all-night convenience store, I bought a phone card, toothbrushes and toothpaste, combs, a hairbrush, and a pair of sharp scissors for my future haircut.

Next, we stopped at a cash station. Both Shirl and I had debit cards in case of emergency, but I'd never expected an emergency like this one. I had fifty pounds left in my wallet, and I decided to withdraw two hundred more. I didn't think I'd disturb Shirl's checking account too much, not that I was spending time worrying about an over-drawn account. I just didn't want the bank to get suspicious and alert anyone. I had a regular charge card but wouldn't use it. Too many characters in suspense movies get caught because of "paper trails." Why take a chance?

Our last stop was a phone booth. We'd talked it over and agreed to try one more time. The phone card took away my worries about not enough change. No answer again at Jean's, so I dialed Dumfrieshire. We'd decided to talk, just briefly, if either Torquil or Fiona-Benita answered. How long would it take to trace a phone call anyway? But again a stranger answered.

"Tell Shirl to trust me," I blurted before hanging up. "She's got to be okay," I whispered. Dennis put his arm around me, and we walked into the station. They were boarding for Edinburgh, but we were able to purchase two seats, though not together. Probably safer that way.

"Staying long in Edinburgh?"

Caught! My heart leaped into my throat. But it was only my seatmate, who'd had enough of her magazine and wanted to chat. I regained my composure, smiled, and shook my head.

"American, aren't you?"

How did she know? I hadn't said anything, and my jumble sale clothes wouldn't give me away.

The large blond girl laughed at my surprise. "I can always tell. Maybe it's because you're holding on to that blanket so tightly. Cold? Just like Cindy. That's one of the girls who joined us. She's from California and starts shivering every evening, too. I'm from Norway. I consider this weather tropical."

I smiled again. I wasn't cold exactly, but the blanket offered comfort. The girl seemed nice, and I wanted to talk to her. But was it a good idea?

"Come on," she said, "be friends. I'm Sonja, like the old skating star. What's your name?"

I thought fast. "Carrie, and you're right. I'm from the States."

"Nice to meet you. I thought you looked a little lost. Do you need a place to stay tonight?"

"No, I'm transferring to another train right away."

"Oh, the sleeper to London. Don't you want to see Edinburgh first?"

"What makes you think I'm going to London?" I asked, both puzzled and amused by Sonja's cocky self-assurance.

"It's the only train still going out tonight. Nothing else leaves until morning."

I must have looked shocked, for she patted my shoulder and made sympathetic noises. "Someone gave you some bad information. It happens. Tell you what, you can come with us."

Sonja explained she was a language student on a backpacking trip through the U.K. and had picked up some traveling companions. "We're all doing the same thing, and it's more fun this way. We couldn't all sit together, though, because we arrived at the station too late and most of the seats were taken. But it turned out well because I met you."

She pointed out her friends as she said their names. "There's me and Cindy, Kevin is from Ireland, and Paul is from France. He doesn't speak much English, but I speak French, so I help him out. We're going to a youth hostel. It doesn't cost much, and," she looked at me sharply, "they don't ask questions. It's near Waverly Station, so you can get an early start tomorrow."

It might not be a bad plan, if Sonja were right that the only train left was going to London. We did not want to go to London! Traveling in a group would make us less noticeable, and we needed places to go where questions weren't asked.

"Thanks. There's one thing, though. I'm not alone either. You see that boy?" I pointed to Denny. "Well, we're together."

"Bring him along," Sonja said grandly. "What's his name?"

I'd anticipated the question. "Dan. Thanks, Sonja. Thanks a lot."

Sonja nodded and pulled another magazine out of her pack.

I put down my blanket and walked past Denny's seat. "Meet me in the buffet car," I murmured. He followed in a few minutes. We propped ourselves against a pole between the two cars and shared a snack while I told him about Sonja.

"Do you trust her?"

"I don't even know her," I said.

We finally agreed, though, to check the train schedule, and if Sonja's information was correct, we'd join her and her friends.

The trip to Edinburgh was short—a little over thirty minutes. In the station, Sonja introduced us to the others, who all seemed rather quiet. Just as well, for Sonja talked non-stop.

"Check the schedules to find out what time you leave tomorrow. We'll wait for you by that door."

Ahead of us at the information booth, I saw an unhappy Betty expressing her need to go to Skye. Someone back in Glasgow had given Betty bad advice, the attendant explained. Didn't she know she could take a train directly from Glasgow to the Kyle of Lochalsh every morning? Crestfallen, Betty walked slowly over to a seat in the waiting area and pulled out a shawl from her worn carpetbag. She looked prepared to stay all night. The wee bairns would have to wait.

Denny and I returned to Sonja. "You're right," I said. "No trains tonight. We leave at eight-thirty tomorrow morning."

Sonja beamed at the entire group. "First, we'll get our rooms, and then we'll take in the sights."

Denny shrugged. "Why not? After all, it is Friday night. We deserve some fun."

*T*he woman thrust Jeanie into a room, so hard that she fell to the floor, and left quickly, locking the door behind her.

At first, Jeanie felt almost grateful to be alone, away from the nasty couple and their endless quarreling. She looked around. It was a nice little cabin, only two rooms—this main one and a bathroom.

Jeanie checked things out. A cot with blankets, a flashlight, a basket of food, and bottles of water. She peeked into the basket: sandwiches, apples, milk, juice, and biscuits. At least they didn't mean to starve her.

When she'd left the car, all she'd seen were woods. She wished now that she'd sat up during the trip. She should have paid attention. But now, she had no idea where she was.

Chapter Sixteen

M IST-COVERED MOUNTAINS I'D EXPECTED, but not mist-covered me. I looked out the train window, unable to see the view from the famous Edinburgh bridge we were crossing. I could hardly even see the bridge. I felt gloomy, and Denny was in an even worse mood—shoulders hunched, hovering over his sketchbook. The body language was clear—no peeking allowed.

Well, I'd take advantage of the silence and get up to date in my journal. But first, I added to my *Things I want to Do* list. *All the sights in Edinburgh*. That should cover it. Then I turned to the day-by-day section.

Sonja and her pals had turned out to be over twenty-one. After we had dinner with them in one pub, we learned their idea of seeing "Edinburgh by night" was to visit all the pubs. Paul even offered "Dan" and me a joint.

Denny shook his head. "Thanks, man, but I've been down that road, and Carrie doesn't even have a map."

"Comment?" Paul raised his brows.

Unlike Paul, I spoke English, but I didn't understand what Denny meant either. What road?

We returned alone to our cheap, though clean, youth hostel. "See you in the morning," I said, before going to the girls' quarters. It felt weird being separated from Denny. Weird and not very safe.

I didn't sleep much, and judging from Denny's appearance the next morning, he didn't either. We arrived at Waverly Station in plenty of time. Then Dennis came up with the brilliant idea that ultimately caused his rotten mood.

"I know how we can help Mom and Shirl."

"How?"

"I'm going to call Dad right now and say they need him. He'll come, all right."

"Denny, it's the middle of the night over there."

"So . . .? At least he'll be home."

Dennis found a phone booth; I stood outside watching him. He was doing more listening than talking, and he looked sad. Did Mr. Ames know something we didn't? Something about Shirl and Liza?

He hung up. "Well?"

"Dad's flying over," Dennis said quietly. "I tried to make him listen, but Mom had already called him and said we'd gotten into some kind of trouble and were missing."

"Some kind of trouble is right," I said. "Well, at least he'll be with them. That makes me feel better."

"He said whatever happened must be my fault." Then Dennis had refused to say any more.

Finally up to date, I looked out the window, searching for "the most beautiful scenery in Scotland," as the guidebooks put it. Gray mist is what I saw. That flash of purple might be heather, but the whole village of Brigadoon could be out there for all I knew. *Take a train ride through the Highlands in clear weather*, I wrote.

"I'm ready for breakfast." I closed the journal. "How about you?"

"Coffee. Black," Dennis said.

Nothing like matching the meal to the mood. "I'll get something sweet, too. You need it." He scowled but swung his knees into the aisle to let me by.

While the buffet attendant filled my breakfast order, I considered how to make Dennis open up—as soon as he finished eating. The weather was depressing enough without him turning back into that unfriendly person I'd first met. There must be some reason his parents were so down on him. They seemed perfectly nice to everyone else.

Dennis only grunted his thanks, but he consumed everything, not just the coffee.

Here goes. I took a deep breath. "Denny, please tell me—what's wrong?"

"Nothing."

"I don't believe you."

He turned on me. "Look Carly, that was a really dumb question. Everything's wrong, remember? Kidnapping, murder, impostors, running from the cops *and* the terrorists. I'm sorry I'm not a happy-go-lucky tourist."

Quite a speech, but I didn't buy it. "You were fine until you called your father. Why are your parents so mean to you?"

Denny had nowhere to hide from my question. He couldn't look out the window; I had the window seat. He looked down at his sketchbook, but it must not have offered enough protection, for he finally turned to me. I could see the pain in his eyes. "Tell me," I said.

"I messed up bad," he said. "Last year, I really let them down."

"What happened?" The sounds of the train, our present situation—everything but Denny—faded in importance.

"I guess it started my sophomore year," he said, finally. "I went through freshman year okay, kind of like a robot, doing what was expected of me. Then I found out about all the art classes Garfield High offered, but Dad said no way."

"You couldn't take any?"

Dennis shook his head. "Nope. Just college prep courses, mainly math and science. I'm supposed to be an engineer, like Dad. But it's not me, Carly."

I agreed.

"After that, I started smoking, let my hair grow, got my ear pierced. I don't even like heavy metal music. I was just trying to bug my parents."

"Major rebellion, and it worked," I said, laughing, although it wasn't funny.

He almost managed a grin. "It sure did." Then he shook his head. "I guess it didn't really. They were more convinced than ever I shouldn't take art. I started hanging out with the 'wrong crowd.' Then last September, I went to this girl's house for a party. Her parents weren't home. I'll bet at least three hundred people showed up. Most of them were drinking and doing drugs. I had a few joints, but I stayed away from the acid and crack—honest. But I was drinking a can of beer when the cops came. The kids who saw the squad cars pull up split out the back way, but I wasn't so lucky."

"And Liza and your dad went ballistic?"

"You got it. I escaped juvenile court but had to do community service and see a substance abuse counselor."

"Gosh," was my brilliant, supportive response. Liza's snide remarks made sense now—also Denny's attitude when we first met. He'd changed, and I suddenly realized how much I'd changed, too. A few weeks ago, I would have totally judged him; now I was trying to understand. What if Shirl was the controlling type? What if she insisted I had to be a teacher like her, instead of taking time to figure out what I wanted? How would I react? But Dennis looked miserable, and I should say something. I put my hand on his.

"That's all ancient history, Denny. You've changed, and your parents will come around."

Denny smiled sadly. "Thanks, Carly. I'll figure out something, once this mess is over. It just hurt when Dad wouldn't even listen—when he automatically blamed me for everything."

We stopped talking. Dennis was still sad, but at least he wasn't shutting me out. I became aware of the sounds of the train again, the clickety-clacks, the swaying, the gentle chugging rhythm . . . When the movement ended, so did my nap. I found my head on Denny's shoulder. I sat up and tried to re-orient myself. "Uh—sorry. Are we there yet?"

"Are we there yet?" Dennis mimicked. "No, just Inverness. Nothing to see—it's still raining. Go back to sleep. I don't mind your using my shoulder for a pillow."

I shook my head at the offer. It was one thing for my head to slip onto Dennis's shoulder by mistake, but quite another to put it there on purpose. I tried to cover my embarrassment. "What do you mean, just Inverness? I can't believe we're not going to stop and look for the Loch Ness Monster." I opened my journal and wrote, *Search for the Loch Ness Monster.*

Dennis leaned over and read the *Things I Want to Do* list. "Allow me," he said, taking my journal. Down both margins, he began sketching little cartoons of all the things I wanted to see. My favorite was a tearful Loch Ness Monster holding an umbrella. Somehow, Denny made it look possible for the monster to have arms and hands. A balloon caption over Nessie's head read, "Come see me, Carly!" Dennis kept me amused with his drawings the rest of the way to the Kyle of Lochalsh.

The rain showed no sign of ending, and I could see nothing but the railway station, which seemed more like a lonely outpost. I felt as if we'd arrived at the end of the world. Inside, we asked a man at the ticket booth where to find the nearest youth hostel.

"I'm afraid yer out of luck. The closest hostel is at Kyleakin on Skye, and the ferry will nae be going there today."

"Because of the rain?" I asked.

"Aye, and the wind. Should clear by tomorrow."

Tomorrow? What about today? "My . . . brother and I need a place to stay. Some place close. We don't have any rain gear."

The man looked displeased. "Ye'll need at least a mac and a brolly here. But the Lochalsh is a grand hotel and only a five minute walk." He sketched a map on a scrap of paper.

I hoped that "grand" didn't mean expensive. I did not want to use the ATM machine again so soon. As we left the station, I noticed a forlorn Betty sitting in the waiting room. Yet another night before she would reach her daughter and grandchildren on the Isle of Skye. I would have given her a hug except she would have thought I was totally nuts.

Five minutes can be endless in pouring rain. Denny and I were drenched by the time we arrived at the Lochalsh Hotel. Sixty-eight pounds a night—plenty expensive, but we had to stay somewhere. I was worried the desk clerk would ask for our passports or refuse to let us stay at all because we were so young, but she accepted the cash. Then I told her we were brother and sister. I didn't think she believed me, but I also didn't think she cared.

Our room was huge. I was relieved to see two double beds and a large private bathroom. Last night, it felt weird being away from Denny. Tonight, it would be weird being with him.

We changed into other jumble sale outfits—sweat pants and polo shirts—and went to the hotel snack bar for food to take back to our room. I picked up tons of tourist pamphlets in the lobby. Might as well have something to read; we weren't going anywhere until the rain stopped.

Denny and I spent the afternoon mostly eating, napping, and drying our clothes. He cut my hair with my new scissors. The results were a bit shaggy but suited me. I looked older and my eyes, huge. I pretended not to notice Denny sticking a lock of my hair into his sketchbook.

As soon as I was satisfied with my "do," I devoured all of the tourist pamphlets. *Pretender to the British Throne: Bonnie Prince Charlie* told how Charles Edward Stewart escaped death at the Battle of Culloden in 1746 and fled to the Isle of Skye. I couldn't wait to see Eilean A'Ceo, as it was called in Gaelic. It meant the Misty Isle. The mist I'd seen already. It was time to see some isle.

Toward evening, I got my wish. I was catnapping when Dennis said, "It's stopped raining. Just look at the view!" I joined him at the window and stared out at dark, still, Loch Alsh and, in the distance, Skye—bleak and mysterious. It was almost worth the whole miserable day to be able to see the view suddenly, all at once.

After our snack machine supper, we decided to explore. Our jackets still weren't dry, so I cut my Black-Watch plaid blanket in half and made ponchos for Denny and me.

We walked hand in hand along the shore, stepping over rocks, picking up shells, but mainly watching the magical rugged land across the water. Day left, but we stayed. We sat on large rock seats and became a silent audience for the sunset show over Skye. Someday, a bridge would replace the ferry, taking people from the mainland to the island, but that evening, the moon laid out another route. It seemed so solid; surely we could simply follow the gleaming path across the loch to reach the Misty Isle. Those without imaginations could rely upon ferries and bridges.

Then Denny turned and kissed me. It wasn't a passionate kiss or even a poetic one. It was just a kiss, but I thought it perfect. I snuggled up next to him, and we continued watching our moon path.

Finally, Denny sighed, then sort of shivered.

"Cold?" I asked. Tenderly, I hoped.

"No." He paused. "Carly, what are we doing?"

I swallowed hard. Was he taking back the kiss? "You mean you don't know?" I tried to keep my voice light—just in case it hadn't meant anything to him.

"Oh, I don't mean us. We're fine. I mean everything else. How long are we going to keep running? Until we have no money and nowhere to run? We'll be caught eventually. Are we going to take the chance that Javier will find us before the cops do?"

He was right. We'd been taking each moment as it came and hadn't thought ahead at all. Why, we were supposed to go home in two days, and our passports were back at the MacNeils'.

"I still have that business card from the U.S. Embassy," I said. "I'll call Curtis Bland tomorrow."

*J*eanie crept under the blankets and covered her head, trying to hide from the real darkness. Another night in this dreadful place. No one, not even her jailers, had come for her. She'd eaten most of her food. Would there be more?

Jeanie had tried every possible way to escape. She'd shouted until she was hoarse. She'd pushed the table under the high window, but even when she stood on her tiptoes and stretched with all her might, she couldn't quite reach.

The two blankets weren't enough tonight; she was cold. Maybe if she threw her mackintosh on top, she'd be warmer. She bolted from the cot and grabbed the coat from its doorknob hanger. To her surprise, a package fell from one of its large pockets.

Oh, right. Aunt Jean had given her a present to open later. Poor Auntie had had no idea where she'd be when later came. Jeanie turned on the precious flashlight and opened the package. Two Chalet School books! Almost as good as more food. She hadn't read either one of them: Volume 12, *The New House at the Chalet School* and volume 21, *Jo to the Rescue.* If only Joey would come to her rescue.

Chapter Seventeen

I MADE THE PHONE CALL after breakfast. "Mr. Bland isn't in his office at the moment," a robot-like woman said, squashing my request. "Would you care to leave a message?"

Not really. Having made the decision, we wanted immediate action. "Uh—what time do you expect him?"

"Wait a minute. Is this Carly Sullivan?" Her voice had changed, and she sounded almost human.

"Yes . . ."

"Carly, Mr. Bland has been hoping you'd call." Her voice dripped honey. "Just give me your number, dear, and I'll have him get in touch with you."

"I don't think so."

Dennis, sitting next to me, started elbow poking. "What's going on?" he whispered. I frowned at him and spoke again into the receiver.

"Uh—could you give me a number instead?" The woman sounded reluctant but did. Torquil's! I hung up, heart pounding.

We talked it over. "You might as well go ahead and call," Denny said. "We don't have much choice."

"Actually, I think I'd rather start life over again on the Isle of Skye—as a permanent babysitter for Betty's grandkids."

"You want me to do it?"

"No, I will." All along I'd done most of the talking. Words were my thing; Denny did the pictures. I dialed.

"MacNeils." Finally a voice I recognized.

"Hello, Torquil. It's me, Carly."

"Carly?" He yelled in my ear. "Carly, do you have Jeanie? Is she with you?"

Before I could answer, I heard commotion on the other end. Then a new voice spoke. "This is Agent Bland, Carly. Do you remember me?"

"Y-es," I acknowledged warily.

"Where are you?"

I stalled. After all, Bland was at Torquil and Fiona-Benita's house, and they were involved in our problems up to their eyelids. First, I'd ask some questions. "Why did you give the newspaper our picture? We didn't murder anyone."

"Is that why you bolted? Because of the newspaper coverage?" Agent Bland sounded disgusted. "I knew it was a mistake. No, you're not in any *legal* trouble. Let's just say we thought it might be better for our side to find you."

Before the other side did, I added silently. Well, better him than the Shining Path. "We're at the Lochalsh Hotel in Kyle of Lochalsh."

He whistled. "My, you do get around. You and Dennis sit tight. It may take me awhile to get there."

"Wait! Has something happened to Jeanie?"

"There have been some problems. I'll fill you in later."

Still, I was reluctant to let him go. "How's my mother?"

"How do you think she is?" he snapped. "Worried sick about you. Wait for me, Carly." He hung up.

"Mr. Bland is coming here," I told Dennis.

"What was that about Jeanie?"

"I don't know. Torquil wondered if she might be with us." It was more than that, though. He hoped she was with us. Neither of us said what we both feared. Had Javier taken Jeanie?

What happened next probably wouldn't have if we'd known how long Curtis Bland would be. Dennis and I packed our few possessions and went outside, trying to find ways to kill time. Both our jackets and our Carly-made ponchos were needed on this dry but crispy-cool day. We were walking up and down the sidewalk, window shopping, when I heard a loud voice I'd never expected to hear again.

"Carrie! Dan! Hoy there!"

Sonja and her gang, which had increased by at least five, charged up the street. They seemed to be coming from the train station. Oddly, I was delighted to see them. Denny and I had run out of small talk, and our fears were too great to share, even with each other. I'm sure he dreaded the reunion with his father, while I felt guilty about Shirl. And both of us were scared to death about Jeanie.

I greeted Sonja & Co. like long lost buddies. "Hi! When did you guys get here?"

"Train just arrived," Sonja said, "and now we're heading for Skye. No place to stay here in our budget." She introduced us to her new followers, whose names and national origins escape me now. They didn't speak much English—no obstacle for Sonja. "We're on our way to the ferry. Want to come along?"

Did I! "What do you say, Den—I mean, Dan. We won't stay long." I turned back to Sonja. "We have to meet some people here later."

Denny shook his head. "Not a good idea. What if Bland comes early and can't find us?"

"But the Isle of Skye! This could be our only chance ever. Even if I can come back someday, the ferry won't be here once the bridge is finished. I want to cross by boat—like Bonnie Prince Charlie."

But Dennis wouldn't budge.

"Don't have all day, kids," Sonja said. "What'll it be?"

"I'm going," I insisted.

Dennis pulled me aside. "Don't you remember Edinburgh? What makes you think they aren't going to do more bar-hopping—or something worse?"

"Don't be silly. That was at night, not morning." I tried pleading. "Oh, come on—just for a little while."

"Sorry. Go ahead if you want, but count me out."

"Fine." I stalked off, blending in perfectly with Sonja's groupies.

I looked back a few times, but Dennis must have returned to the hotel. I felt awful about quarreling with him, but why did he have to be so unreasonable?

Since we were traveling on foot, we stood on the deck of the ferry, although plenty of people left their cars below to join us. I felt such a thrill. Of course I knew this wasn't the actual spot where Bonnie Prince Charlie had crossed over to Skye, and even if it were, he certainly never traveled by ferry. But I had a good imagination, and I used it.

I moved away from the crowd, looked over toward the Misty Isle, and sang *The Skye Boat Song*. Fortunately, the sounds of the wind drowned me out. I could be as sentimental as I wished.

> *Speed bonnie boat like a bird on the wing,*
> *Onward the sailors cry.*
> *Carry the lad that was born to be king,*
> *Over the sea to Skye.*

Shirl used to sing that to me when I was a little girl. I remembered asking once if her friend Fiona had taught it to her. "No, Fiffy didn't know any Scottish folk songs," Shirl had said, "but she taught us some Peruvian ones."

As soon as I had the chance, I'd add that to my Fiona in the 70s list. Fiona didn't know Scottish songs. More proof she wasn't who she said she was. Wait a minute . . . I was getting mixed up. Who wasn't who she said she was? A picture of Fiona at the ceilidh in Dumfries flashed into my mind—Fiona of today, knowing all the words to the songs, not just the chorus. I was confused. Nothing made sense, unless . . . Oh, my God! What if . . .?

We reached the Kyleakin shore. I walked off, still in a daze over my incredible thought, and hardly reacted to Sonja's words. "Let's check out the hostel. Then we'll hitch a ride and see what kind of pubs this island has to offer."

"Not me, thanks," I said. "I'll take a look at the castle, and then go back on the ferry."

"Well, have fun," Sonja said. "Maybe we'll see you later." They waved gaily and left me alone on the pier, preparing for what seemed like an easy hike.

The *Caisteal Maol,* a turretless ruin, overlooked the pier. According to one of my tourist pamphlets, the castle had been built by a Danish princess nicknamed Saucy Mary, who stretched a chain across the narrows of the kyle—the body of water between the island and the mainland—and refused to let any ship pass unless it paid a toll. The castle was farther away than it looked, and the way up was steep. I soon grew breathless climbing over the rocks, which stood like medieval guards surrounding the castle.

Stopping to rest, I pulled out my journal and reviewed my Fiona lists. Fiona in the 70s had been vivacious, charismatic, and headstrong. She spoke with a strong Spanish accent and, although her parents were Scots and only employed in Peru, she knew no Scottish folk songs. She was a poor to average student. Because of a botched abortion, she was unable to have children. Fiona of today was vivacious, charismatic, and practical. She spoke in a cultured British accent and knew many Scottish folk songs. She was a successful child psychologist, wife, and mother. Okay, if you had to name these girls, which one would be Fiona Douglas, and which one would be Benita Velasco? My answer was troublesome and only raised more questions.

Time to get moving. I could see someone down below beginning the climb. Could it be Denny? No! I turned and clambered up the rocks as fast as I dared, followed by Mr. No-name, whom I'd last seen with Javier, trailing Kent Travis from the Old Vic Theatre!

I had a good head start and would find a place to hide in the ruins. I flung off my poncho and kept on scrambling. Soon my hands were scraped and bleeding—probably my knees, too. Why didn't you stay with Dennis, you idiot? No, I'd scold myself later.

Just when I thought I could go no farther, I heard a booming voice that sounded like it came from a megaphone. "Carly Sullivan, this is Harold Miggs, British Intelligence. It's all over. Come on down."

Yeah, right. I felt a new surge of energy and continued the climb to Saucy Mary's.

He spoke again. "You can stop running, Carly. We arrested Javier Estaban yesterday, in Glasgow."

That made me pause. I wanted to believe him. But he hadn't stopped Javier from murdering Kent. How trustworthy could he be? I scrambled on.

Another voice. "Carly, this is Agent Bland. Agent Miggs is telling the truth. He was working undercover. Come down. Dennis Ames is here with us."

Then why didn't they let him talk? But there were three figures. One might be Dennis, but I couldn't tell for sure, or if he were there by choice. As for me, I had no choice now. I couldn't leave Denny alone with killers, and I didn't think there was help for me up ahead.

The castle looked deserted. Maybe if I went down, pretending to cooperate, I could make a run for it and find help in the village. "Okay, I'm coming," I shouted, and made my descent.

As soon as I reached flat land, I angled off to the side and started running—faster than I'd ever run before—toward the pier where there were people. I was gasping so hard I could scarcely breathe. My throat and lungs burned. Everything hurt. I heard the men running, too, calling after me to stop. But I wouldn't until I could find someone who'd listen. Exhausted and bleeding, I kept on, even though I knew my chances of getting help were slim. I mean, who would believe me? My word against the CIA and British Intelligence? Then just before I reached the pier, I tripped and fell. There were people on the pier, but instead of helping, they looked at me as if I were some oddity and turned away. It was over, as Mr. Miggs had said.

"Carly!" It was the voice I needed to hear. "It's all right. They're telling the truth!"

Denny came up to me alone while the two men stood back and watched. He helped me up and held me close. "Everything's all right, Carly. Everything's all right," he soothed as if I were a small child, until Bland and Miggs joined us.

Someone on the pier must have reported the disturbance, for a policeman appeared and asked if I needed assistance. Miggs pulled out a card, though, that caused the policeman to practically salute before he made a hasty exit. Denny had better be right about them.

My spirits and some of my energy started to return. Mostly I felt angry and didn't care who the men were. "For heaven's sake," I practically sobbed, "why didn't you let Dennis talk to me over your loudspeaker? Did you really think I'd trust you?"

Bland shook his head. "We've made mistakes."

They weren't getting off that easily. "I saw you," I said quietly to Miggs. "You were with Javier when he killed Kent Travis."

"You don't hold back, do you?" Agent Miggs chuckled—ruefully, I thought. "Carly, we would have handled things differently if we'd realized you knew so much. I never expected Javier to pull out a knife, much less use it. If I had objected, you would have found two dead bodies."

"Why did you give the newspaper our pictures? The ones I drew?" Dennis was upset, too.

"Javier saw you that night," Miggs explained. "He decided to get rid of you. You needed protection, but Bland and I couldn't locate you anywhere; you'd left London. We didn't know then you were connected with the MacNeils. We were afraid Javier would find you before we did, so we asked the police and the newspapers for help."

My anger faded. "Javier really has been arrested?"

"Yes," Miggs said. "I was just waiting for definite proof to connect him to a terrorist group."

"S.L.," I interjected, giving the acronym for Sendero Luminoso.

"Uh—yes." Agent Miggs *hadn't* given us much credit. "Dennis's sketch gave us our first positive identification. We arrested him, but now I wonder if we shouldn't have waited longer."

He meant Jeanie.

"Jeanie?" Dennis said, echoing my thought.

Bland nodded soberly. "Abducted by a man and woman who answered your descriptions. The Glasgow police made the connection with your picture in the newspaper and called Scotland Yard. The Yard contacted us. Javier was arrested, though, before we found out Jeanie hadn't disappeared with you."

"Javier must have hired the kidnappers," Miggs continued, "but he hasn't talked yet."

"He won't," Dennis said.

I'd also read enough about the Senderistos to agree. Javier would admit nothing. I sat on the ground and pulled Denny next to me. We huddled close. The agents walked away, talking. Leaving us out again, I supposed, but I no longer cared. I wanted soap and warm water and Shirl, and I needed to speak to Denny in private.

"I'm sorry I was such a spoiled brat," I whispered. "I should have stayed with you, but I didn't think Bland would come so fast."

"You are a brat," Denny whispered back, but he kissed me on top of my head. "They came by helicopter, and that's how we're going back to Dumfries."

"Wow!" Optimistic Carly had returned.

Before we boarded the helicopter that stood waiting in an open field outside of Kyleakin, Agent Bland called Torquil. "There's been a ransom note," Bland said, as soon as he hung up his cellphone.

"What did it say?" Miggs asked.

Agent Bland read from his notebook. "Return to Peru what is hers. Your daughter in exchange for the Velasco diamonds."

*A*ll day long, Jeanie fought off panic. She tried to practice self-discipline, as the teachers at school suggested. She pretended to be in an air-raid shelter during the Blitz, just like Grandmother MacNeil had been. She even put herself on a strict rationing program. She could read a chapter in one of the Chalet School books. After that, she had to do push-ups or run in place. Then she allowed herself a little bread or fruit and a tiny sip of water. But sometimes, Jeanie just had to stop and cry. What would she do when her food and water were gone?

<h1 style="font-family:cursive">Chapter Eighteen</h1>

T HE HELICOPTER RIDE TO DUMFRIESHIRE was quick but incredible. Better than any amusement ride I'd ever been on. I didn't have time to do much more than jot messily into my journal, *Tour the Isle of Skye*, before grabbing Denny's arm and gaping at Scotland sliding by beneath us.

We landed in a field on the MacNeil estate and were met by Torquil and Dennis's father, John Ames. Mr. Ames didn't even bother to get out of the van. At least Torquil welcomed the men. He shook hands and muttered things I couldn't make out. We piled into the van and still Denny and I were ignored. I mean, not a "Thank goodness you're back," or "Are you hungry, thirsty, tired?" Not even "How dare you run off and worry your poor mothers?" Nothing! Sure, we'd made mistakes, but I couldn't understand why we were being treated like naughty children.

The front door of hacienda MacNeil opened as our van pulled into the drive. Three women came out on the porch and stood waiting. As soon as the van stopped, I jumped out, away from the judging atmosphere, and did something completely out of character. "Mother," I yelled, and charged up the front steps. I hurled myself into Shirl's arms and burst out crying. She cried, too.

"Oh, Carly, thank God you're safe!" Finally someone cared.

As we all gathered in the lounge, I looked hard at Shirl. She was in terrible shape—face drawn and pale, clothes and hair like an unmade bed. "Carly, your hair?" she said, as we sat close together on a floral-print settee.

"Like it?" I felt my sense of humor returning.

"It's . . . different," Shirl acknowledged.

"So was my hairdresser. What about Denny's haircut? Doesn't he look great?" No response from anyone. "He quit smoking," I added helpfully.

Dennis stood alone near a window, as far from his parents as possible. A clam-silent Liza and the forbidding John Ames sat on another settee across from us. I thought Liza had reacted to my remarks about Dennis, but she crawled back into her shell when her husband put his hand on hers and shook his head.

Fiona, who didn't look rested or well groomed either, stood in the doorway to the kitchen, instructing sorrowful Nanny to bring in tea. The agents and Torquil had gathered around a desk, presumably to study the ransom note.

"Agatha Christie!" I blurted out. Everyone stared at me as if I'd finally gone over the top. "You know," I said sheepishly, "at the end of her books, all the suspects gather in a room like this and tell what they know. Then the detective puts the clues together and announces who's guilty. Don't you think that's a good idea?"

John Ames glared at me. "Young lady, you and my son seem to think this is a game designed especially for your amusement. Have you any idea the mess you've created?"

We've created? What are you talking about? I wanted to say, but Mr. Ames was overwhelming. I kept quiet. Poor Denny—having such a father.

But Dennis must have decided to stop being poor. "Stop," he said. His voice wasn't loud exactly, but it . . . projected, as play directors say. It carried authority, and we all watched as he crossed the room toward his father.

"Stop blaming Carly and me. We didn't kidnap or murder anyone. We're not thieves or impostors, either." Fiona gasped, but Denny didn't seem to notice. "The minute we landed in London, people started jerking us around. Torquil even had us kidnapped so we wouldn't meet his wife. Yeah, we figured it out," he said, as Torquil's mouth dropped and Bland and Miggs exchanged glances. "Then when we reported what happened, everyone at the U.S. Embassy blew us off." Miggs stood up, but Bland gestured for him to sit down again. "Finally," Dennis concluded, "when we followed the kidnappers and Agent Miggs from the theater, we found Kent Travis murdered."

"So you did think I was involved," Agent Miggs said.

"Is that why you waited so long to contact me? Because you thought I was in on it, too?" Agent Bland asked.

Dennis nodded.

"Makes sense, doesn't it?" I said.

"Then what happened?" Shirl urged, so I took up the story.

"Dennis and I decided to do some research at the library in Glasgow. That's where we found out about the Shining Path and . . . uh . . . something else. We were waiting for Torquil when we saw our picture on the front page of the newspaper. Maybe we shouldn't have run, but Torquil was so late . . . Well, we freaked out. About more than the newspaper picture, too. We'd read something at the library that made us think Javier might be a Senderisto. And he *had* followed us to Glasgow."

"You couldn't miss him," Denny added. "He and Torquil almost crashed into each other on the highway."

"Why didn't you tell me about him then?" Torquil demanded.

"We don't trust kidnappers," Dennis said. That silenced him.

"We tried to call your sister's house," I said. "No one was home. Probably you were at the police station already, but we didn't know about Jeanie then. And later when we tried to call you, we could tell the line was bugged."

"So you hung up and ran." Mr. Ames sneered. "Of all the juvenile stunts."

Agent Miggs moved closer. "I don't agree, sir. Actually, their 'stunts' probably saved their lives. Possibly young Jeanie's too." Mr. Ames finally looked less sure of himself. Miggs explained, "If you hadn't left Glasgow, Javier would have had you abducted and killed. First framing you for Jeanie's disappearance, of course. Carly and Dennis threw him off kilter. He had no idea where they were, and he became careless."

"This isn't helping find my daughter," Fiona said.

Denny pulled the photocopied picture from his backpack. "What's wrong, Benita? Afraid of the truth?"

"I don't know what you mean," she said, her voice shaking.

"Sure you do." He handed the picture of the Velasco family to Curtis Bland. "Meet Benita Velasco, everyone. She's impersonating Fiona Douglas. Probably has been for years."

Shirl stiffened next to me, and I held my breath, watching Fiona. I was pretty sure what she would say.

The tiny woman shook her head. "You're wrong," she said quietly. "I'm exactly who I say I am. But you've been right about one thing, Shirl. I never went to college with you. That girl was Benita Velasco. Benita was the impostor."

Everyone gasped but me—I just nodded. I'd figured it out while crossing to the Isle of Skye. Everything Shirl had told me about her college friend indicated a strong Spanish background. But Mrs. MacNeil was Scottish to the core.

Torquil put his arm around Fiona. "Can't this wait until we find our daughter," he pleaded.

Curtis Bland shook his head. "It might sound foolish, but I'm inclined to go along with Carly's Agatha Christie scenario. Kidnapping, impersonation—these are serious charges. I think we'd better hear Mrs. MacNeil's story."

I felt sorry for Fiona. "It might help Jeanie if we all tell what we know."

"Please," Shirl said, "I need to hear what happened."

Nanny brought in tea and set it on the coffee table. Fiona, Torquil, and the two agents arranged themselves on the other settees. Dennis squeezed in next to me.

Slowly, Fiona poured milk into her cup before adding tea. Finally, she dropped in one cube of sugar and stirred much longer than necessary.

"We're waiting," Liza said—the first words I'd heard from her since we'd returned.

Fiona gave a great sigh. "It's a long story," she said.

*J*eanie sang practically every song she knew. Pops's favorite, "Haste Ye Back," only made her cry, so she tried cheerful songs with lots of verses: "Three Crows Sat Upon a Wall," "The Wee Cooper O' Fife," "The Laird O' Cockpen," "The Barnyards of Delgaty." She even sang "I've Been Working on the Railroad," and the entire "12 Days of Christmas"—twice.

Her food was gone, so Jeanie read her second Chalet School book, and waited.

Chapter Nineteen

FIONA TWISTED HER WEDDING BAND. "As most of you know, my father left Scotland after university and went to Peru to be a copper miner with his college friend, Carlos Velasco Alvarado. Carlos was Juan Velasco's younger brother."

I dropped four lumps of sugar into my cup. Did Fiona have to go back that far?

"Shortly after Father arrived in Lima, he met and married my mother, who was from England. I was born in Lima. My father wanted to give me a Spanish name, but Mother wanted to keep me as true to my heritage as possible."

"Is all this really necessary?" John Ames echoed my thought. Liza put her hand on his and frowned.

"Sorry, I'll move on." Fiona continued. "In 1968, shortly after my fifteenth birthday, Juan Velasco, who had become a powerful general, led a coup—a military overthrow of the government—and took power. My father still worked for the copper mine, but now he worked for Velasco, too. They'd been close friends for years. My mother hated him, though I didn't know why at the time."

Fiona stood and walked over to the window. We had to strain to hear her next words. "Velasco took power in October. Mother died in December. She'd never been very strong. After that, Father started taking me to the Governor's Palace with him. And I met Benita Velasco."

Finally! "And she looked exactly like you," I guessed.

Fiona smiled faintly and returned to her seat. "Not exactly, although the resemblance was remarkable. Benita was seventeen, two years older than I. We were identical in height, though, and people often said they had trouble telling our voices apart, especially our laughter. She wore her hair different from mine, and her eyes were a different color—green. No wait, I'll explain in a bit," Fiona said, as Shirl started to object. "Our personalities, though, were poles apart. I was quiet and oh so proper, but Benita was the liveliest, most daring girl I'd ever met."

Shirl and Liza nodded, remembering.

"Nanny became upset every time Father took me to the palace. She shared Mother's hatred of Velasco, although I think she was just being faithful to Mother's memory. I believe now that Benita must have been my half-sister."

"Half-sister!" Shirl exclaimed.

"It would explain the resemblance—we both looked like Mother. It also would explain my mother's feelings, if he'd rejected her and taken away her first daughter. I have no proof, but it's a reasonable theory, I think."

"Did you like Benita?" I asked, hoping to get the story moving again. I couldn't believe how patient the agents were being.

"Yes, I liked her well enough, and I enjoyed going to dinner at an important place like the Governor's Palace. But other than missing

Mother, my life went on very much as before. I was a good student, and I decided I wanted to go to the U.S. to university. Father agreed to send me, and we sent for catalogues and applications. It was one of the proudest moments of my life when I was accepted . . ." Her voice faded. I began to guess what was coming and could feel a knot forming in my chest.

"But you never got to go," Shirl said. For the first time, she sounded sorry for Fiona.

Fiona shook her head, smiling sadly. "By 1971, Velasco had made many enemies, and his family began receiving death threats. He became paranoid with fear. He was terrified, especially for Benita, and had her guarded around the clock. Benita must have been wild being under what amounted to house arrest, so what happened next might have been her idea. It will be hard for you to understand what my father did. I understand now. Perhaps someday I will even be able to forgive."

We leaned forward in anticipation.

"Shirl, Liza—do you remember what Benita was like? How she could talk you into doing things you never ever would have done on your own?"

Shirl and Liza nodded gravely.

"Juan Velasco was like that—even more so than Benita. My father was immersed in Velasco's personality. So he listened while Velasco talked him into robbing me of my dream and even my identity."

Tears came to my eyes. I couldn't help it. When I reached out for Denny's hand, I noticed him looking at his father a little more kindly. Mr. Ames was a saint compared to Fiona's father.

"The last time I saw Benita Velasco, she had my short, curly permed hair and wore contact lenses the color of my eyes. 'What a lark it will be,' she said in Spanish. 'I plan to be a very fine Fiffy indeed.' She even took the nickname Mother had given me."

"Where did you go?" Liza asked. "You were in danger, too, looking so much like Benita."

"I was. Nanny and I were disguised and sent to Ayacucho, one of the poorest parts of the country, where no one would think of looking for a general's or even a successful miner's daughter. We lived with a widow and her son in a primitive shack that lacked plumbing and electricity. That the boy was my age worried Nanny greatly. But the boy didn't care about girls. He was very bright and had a full scholarship at a university in a nearby town. All he could talk about was his professor, who was going to start a new world order in Peru."

Denny squeezed my hand tightly. "Sendero Luminoso," he breathed.

"You did study at the library," Fiona said appreciatively. "Yes, the professor started the Shining Path, although the world wouldn't take it seriously until almost ten years later. The boy's name was Javier Estaban."

No one spoke, but I could hear the sound of a great breath expelled from everyone in the room. So much explained, but so much still a puzzle. "Did you have to stay there all four years—while Benita took your place?"

"Fortunately, no," Fiona continued. "After several months, Nanny and I left by ship and docked eventually in Liverpool, where we went to live with my grandparents."

"And then to college—I mean university, in England?" I suggested.

Fiona shook her head. "My grandparents didn't believe in higher education for women."

"Then how—" I started, but Shirl stopped me.

"Don't ask so many questions, Carly. Let Fiona explain in her own way."

Fiona smiled her thanks. Somewhere during the story, they had become friends. "My father stayed in Peru. Shortly after Benita graduated in 1975 and returned home, Velasco was replaced, supposedly for reasons of ill health. Then Velasco and my father disappeared. I never saw either of them again. Father did send me a trunk, though, which contained, among other things, Benita's diaries of her college years, her photo album, and her diploma."

"So that's how you knew about us," Liza said.

"Not enough, I'm afraid. Shirl suspected me from the very beginning."

Benita must have left certain things out of her diaries—like an abortion, for instance. I wondered why Fiona had even invited us here. Perhaps she still was trying to make up for those lost college years. I tuned back into the conversation.

"But what about Fif—I mean Benita? Where is she now?"

"I'm truly sorry, Shirl," Fiona said. "Your friend was murdered at the Governor's palace, shot by one of the servants. It happened in 1975."

"Oh, no!" Shirl started to sob.

"Shirl," Liza said. "Look at it this way. We always wondered why she never wrote to us. Don't you see? She would have written if she could. I'm sure she never stopped caring about us."

Shirl nodded but kept on crying, quietly now. We were drained—all of us. My muscles ached, and a bathroom break would soon be crucial. How much longer would we be sitting, listening?

Agent Bland cleared his throat. I'd almost forgotten he was in the room. "We really need to tie this up. This is one of the most astounding stories I've ever heard, but did you really need to have these people abducted?" He gestured toward the Moms, Dennis, and me.

Torquil stood and walked behind the settee. He put his hand on Fiona's shoulder and looked prepared to deliver a tale every bit as long and weird as hers. "I didn't learn about Fiona's past until last February when two things happened."

Fiona reddened, and I guessed that it hadn't been very pleasant for her when Torquil had found out.

"First, we were robbed, and the only things missing were diaries, photograph albums, and costume jewelry. Fiona told me not to call the police, that things were more complicated than they appeared. Then she told me the whole story, and that's when I hired Travis Kent."

"And somehow, Kent traced the robbery to Javier and learned his identity," Miggs interjected. "British Intelligence suspected Javier of illegal activities—possibly drugs—and I had managed to strike up an acquaintance with him. But we didn't know his true identity until we saw Dennis's sketch. It was Javier who introduced me to Kent Travis. Perhaps Travis was murdered for attempting blackmail. More likely, though, Javier didn't want anyone in England to know of his connection to the Shining Path."

"What else happened in February?" Bland spoke sharply. Maybe he was annoyed the Agatha Christie game was taking so long.

"A magazine that published an article of mine sent me Shirl's letter," Fiona said. "My secretary didn't show it to me, though, until February, several months after it had been written and after invitations to Shirl and Liza had already been sent."

"Fiona was terrified of meeting you," Torquil said, "and I was afraid you might be involved in the robbery. It seemed such a coincidence, the two events occurring so close together."

"Afraid of us? Why, Fiona?" Liza asked.

"I took Benita's degree. I'd studied alone for over four years and, after my grandparents' death, I took entrance exams and went to graduate school. I used Benita's transcripts and undergraduate degree."

"Benita didn't do you any favors," Liza observed. "She was a terrible student."

Fiona smiled ruefully. "I did have to work very hard to convince people I could succeed, but I did, finally, and on my own merits. I've always worried, though, that a scandal over my past would destroy my career as well as Torquil's. People in my country are so fond of scandals."

"But the robbery," Mr. Ames said. "What was the Shining Path after? Surely not costume jewelry and old diaries and pictures."

"The Velasco diamonds," I breathed. They did sound romantic.

"I don't know," Fiona said. "I'd never heard of them until the ransom note came."

Harold Miggs offered an explanation. "When Velasco and your father disappeared, many valuables disappeared with them, including a large quantity of priceless diamonds. Finding them would have made Javier a full-fledged Sendero Luminoso hero. I wonder whatever became of them . . ."

I caught a curious expression on Fiona's face. Could it be? I looked around at this magnificent room, really looked, and then I thought about the grandness of the MacNeils' entire lifestyle. Suddenly, I had a strong suspicion. That trunk Fiona had received containing Benita's things . . . Fiona's father had sent the Velasco diamonds to her—as a way of making amends. And why not? Who deserved them more than Fiona, after what had been done to her? It wasn't as if the diamonds would be used to help the poor people of Peru. The diamonds couldn't even bring Jeanie back now.

"So you hired Kent Travis to kidnap us so we couldn't expose Fiona," Dennis said to Torquil.

"At the time I didn't think of it as kidnapping, but yes, I paid Kent to . . . delay you."

"That he did," Liza said. "He even pulled a gun on us."

"I didn't anticipate that." Torquil sounded apologetic.

"And Javier drove the car," Dennis added.

"I never paid much attention to the man," Torquil said defensively. "I thought he was just Travis's driver. I don't even know where he took you."

My brain, which had been sorting and sifting through back files, suddenly completed its work and retrieved what was needed. "I've got it! I'm almost positive I know where Jeanie is." I reached into my backpack and pulled out one of the few purchases I'd made in England. *Bath and Environs*, the geological survey map. "Get your sketchbook, Denny. We're going back to Limpley Stoke." Agatha Christie would have been proud of me.

*F*or *the third night in* a row, a huddled form gave shape to the two blankets covering a flimsy cot. The only light, a weak one indicating an ailing battery, had been turned off. Little sounds interrupted the silence: shallow breaths, a tummy gurgling, and the whimpered words, "Mummy, I want Mummy."

Chapter Twenty

I T WOULD BE EASIER TO locate the cottage if we traveled the same route we'd taken before, so we left for London via Glasgow Airport—the agents, Torquil, Mr. Ames, Denny, and me. Shirl, Liza, and Mr. Ames didn't want us to go, but we managed to convince them. "Denny and I may be the only ones who can find the cottage," I said. The only useless member of our team was John Ames. "Why is he coming?" I whispered to Denny.

"To watch me, of course."

We left Shirl and Liza comforting Fiona, who didn't feel well. She was wiped out—both from revealing her long, sad story and her fear for Jeanie.

The sun went down just as we landed in London. Agent Bland rented two cars for our large rescue team, but the men decided not to attempt the drive to Limpley Stoke until morning. I didn't have a vote, of course, but inside I agreed. Dennis and I would need daylight and sharp, rested minds to find our way back to where we'd been held captive.

At our hotel, we gathered in a lounge the agents had secured to study the map and sketchbook. We fortified ourselves with sodas, beer for the men, and crisps. "Show me again where you saw the guard." Bland referred to a sketch Denny had made of the cottage and the surrounding woods. Dennis pointed to where we saw him from our tabletop lookout.

"We think the other guard waited in back," I said.

The plan was for Miggs, Dennis, and his father to approach the rear of the cottage while Bland and Torquil tackled the front. Both agents had guns. They expected me to stay in the car.

I suggested a minor adjustment to the plan. "I should be with Denny. What if the kidnappers make a run for it and use the car I'm in for a get-away? I'd be a hostage."

Torquil grinned. "We'll lock you inside and take the key," he said. "No, lassie, you'll do your part by finding the cottage and then by being patient."

Before we went to our rooms, Miggs started browsing through the sketchbook. He stopped suddenly at a picture of Sonja and her gang. "Who are these people?"

I explained. "The last time I saw them was in Kyleakin just before you found me. They were planning to hitch rides and see the rest of Skye."

Miggs punched some numbers into his phone. "Harris," he said, "I've got a lead on your Irish runaway. He was last seen this morning on Skye, traveling with a large group of students. That's right. I've got a detailed sketch and will fax you a copy. Cheers." Miggs turned to Dennis. "May I?"

Denny sat silent, slowly shaking his head.

I grabbed the sketchbook. "For heaven's sake, Denny." I tore the sketch out of the book and handed it to Miggs. Denny didn't get mad. He just couldn't do it himself.

I remembered the Irish boy. His name was Kevin. He didn't talk much, but neither did the others except . . . I had a disturbing thought. "The rest of the students won't be in trouble, will they?" I meant Sonja. I felt certain she wouldn't have betrayed us.

"Not likely," Miggs said, "though we may run a check on all of them. Don't worry about it, Carly. This boy has caused his parents unbelievable misery."

After Miggs left, Bland thumbed through the sketchbook. "Dennis, I have many experienced artists working for me, but none of them can approach this. What are you planning to do now that you've graduated high school?"

Denny opened his mouth to answer, but his father supplied the words. "He'll go to the University of Wisconsin in Madison—on probation." He made probation sound like a dirty word.

"Probation, why?" Torquil asked.

"Low math and science scores," Denny mumbled.

Bland looked confused. "You need to be good in math and science for art school?"

"Dennis is going to be an engineer." Mr. Ames stuck out his chin.

"Is that what you want, lad?" Torquil asked.

Denny squirmed and looked at his shoes. Wasn't he going to say anything? Tell him, Denny, I thought as hard as I could. Tell him now.

Although it was Torquil who'd asked the question, Denny gave the answer to his father. "No, I don't want to be an engineer. I've never wanted to be one. I'd like to be a sketch artist and work with the police to find criminals and missing people." There! He'd said it!

John Ames turned white but kept silent. Probably thought it was beneath his dignity to make a scene in front of strangers. He was wearing this wait-until-I-get you-alone expression. I was glad Denny was sharing a room with Torquil as well as his father.

Agent Bland whistled. "It appears I've uncovered a land mine," he said, "so maybe we'd better call it a night. But Dennis, you have a gift. I hope you'll think about how you're going to use it." He left the room without acknowledging John Ames.

Torquil escorted me to my room. "Don't you worry about Denny," he said quietly. "I'll be the referee. There's nothing I wouldn't do for the two people who will take me to my Jeano-Beano." His mouth quivered, and his eyes filled.

I got into bed, but my brain was too muddled for sleep. Everyone just assumed we'd find Jeanie and she'd be okay. What if everyone, including me, was wrong?

The next morning it rained. "Same as our first morning in London," I informed Agent Bland at breakfast. "It was raining when we were kidnapped and taken to the cottage."

The others joined us. Such a difference in Denny. Smiling, self-assured, he gave me a big hug and didn't seem to mind who was watching. "It's just possible," he said, as we went out to the cars, "that I'll be staying and studying art in Scotland."

"Really? What happened?"

Denny waited until everyone else started to get into the cars. "Torquil offered to pay my tuition at Glasgow U. Dad wouldn't stand for that. He said . . ." Denny imitated his father. "'I'll need to think about it, but no one pays for my son but me.'"

I chuckled as Denny and I got into the back seat. For once, his father's pride might help him. I glanced at Mr. Ames, sitting next to Agent Bland, who was driving our car. He looked defeated. But I didn't feel sorry for him.

I did feel sorry for me, that is, if Denny remained. I'd sort of figured he'd be part of my life from now on. We'd see each other on weekends, and there would be Homecoming and Senior Prom—stuff like that. As for staying in Scotland, I was the one who'd fallen in love with the country, not Denny.

"Look, Carly, there's the sign that told us we were going in the wrong direction—the sign to London." After that, I forgot about my own small troubles and concentrated on the road and on finding Jeanie.

We got lost a few times. Once we pulled into the wrong country lane. "I told you it was too soon," Denny scolded me. "You were still asleep when we drove past here."

And once we became separated from the second car, so we pulled over to the side until Torquil realized his mistake and found us. "Too bloody bad we don't have my van," he shouted out the driver's window.

Finally, both Denny and I agreed. "This is it," he said. "This is where Javier turned off."

We'd already decided two cars couldn't just drive up to the front door of the cottage. We found a place where we could pull off and be reasonably hidden by trees. "This is where we leave you, Carly," Curtis Bland said.

They started walking down the road. I guess they were filled with the spirit of adventure, for only Bland remembered me. He made sure the car doors were locked and gave me a thumbs up before joining the rest of the group.

I watched them disappear from sight. And I waited. I must have thought about something, but I don't recall what. My brain became blank, and I felt numb. Finally, I looked at my watch. Only ten minutes—was that all? I flung open the car door, remembering to push the button so the door would lock behind me. I would not supply the get-away car.

The rain had almost stopped as I walked down the deserted road in my best Nancy Drew manner. All I lacked was the magnifying glass. The cottage should be around the next bend. I began ducking cautiously behind each tree. I went on this way, from tree to tree until . . . yes, there it was—the cottage where Javier and Kent had taken us. And there at the front door were Torquil, Dennis, and the two agents. Mr. Ames sat on the fallen log our guard had used as his post. I rushed over to him. "Did they find Jeanie?"

"She is inside," he said, "but they can't get the door open. It's padlocked shut. And the windows are too high to reach. Who would design such a house?"

I shrugged.

"The cabin isn't old, and it's constructed in such an odd manner. It makes me wonder if it were designed to restrain people—to be a prison."

"You could be right," I said, warming toward him slightly.

"The kidnappers appear to have gone. If it weren't for you, the child might not have been discovered in time. She would have died of starvation."

"You mean if it weren't for Dennis," I said, not trusting myself to say more. I hurried over to the others. "Can't you just shoot off the lock?"

"You were supposed to wait," Agent Miggs said. "Oh, never mind, it doesn't matter now. Yes, we thought about using a gun, but we don't want to make too much noise in case someone is still around. I'm going into the village for a ladder."

"Is Jeanie all right?"

"She will be once we get her out. You're fine, aren't you, sweetheart?" Torquil called up toward the high window.

"Yes, but hurry, please," a little voice answered.

"Hi, Jeanie," I shouted.

Tears came to my eyes when I heard her faint reply. "Hi, Carly."

"They're going for a ladder, Jeanie," Dennis said.

"Ask them to bring water—and food." She sounded hoarse.

Denny, Torquil, and I looked at each other in horror. Had she been without food and water this whole time?

"We need to get her out of there. Now!" Torquil said. "Do something!"

"Do you know when the kidnappers might return, lassie?" Miggs shouted.

"They're gone. They said they were leaving the country in an airplane. I think it was two nights ago."

Bland and Miggs nodded to each other. Quickly, Miggs moved away from the cottage and pulled out his mobile, possibly to alert the airports, while Bland reached for his gun. "Stand far away from the door, Jeanie," Bland ordered. "I'm going to blow off the lock."

It was over in an instant, and we all cheered as little Jeanie rushed into her father's arms. Torquil held her tightly and whispered something into her ear. Then she turned and spoke to us.

"Thank you very much for rescuing me," she said primly, like a well-brought-up child thanking people for coming to her birthday party.

"It was our pleasure," Agent Bland said. Some of us had tears in our eyes.

It seemed safer to leave immediately. Besides, Jeanie wanted to get far away from the cottage. I felt the same way.

After Torquil contacted everyone waiting back in Dumfrieshire, we began the long drive back. He decided that would be a calmer way for Jeanie to return to reality than having to face the hustle and confusion of Heathrow Airport. Torquil drove, with Mr. Ames as his silent front-seat companion. Denny and I sat in the back with Jeanie, who ate, sipped water, and talked the entire trip.

"And I sang and played games and read and . . ." Jeanie chattered on.

"You are one of the two bravest girls I've ever known," Denny said, squeezing my hand to tell me I was the other one.

John Ames turned and looked at his son. Then he asked if he could see the sketchbook. For most of the trip back, he studied it, occasionally glancing over his shoulder at Dennis. Shortly before we arrived, he returned it. "You may stay here, Dennis," was all he said.

We had a grand reunion, as the Scots would say. We cried a little and hugged a lot. Fiona and Nanny wouldn't stop fussing over Jeanie, who finally escaped, announcing that she needed to go to her room to make sure no one had taken her dolls.

Torquil and Mr. Ames informed Liza and Fiona of the change in Dennis's plans, and I left them arguing over whether he should go to university in Glasgow or Edinburgh.

Alone, I wandered over to Cairlaverock Castle, pleased to find something that had stayed the same. Our plane tickets had been changed. We'd leave from Glasgow rather than London, though we would go home the next day as planned. John Ames would return in Denny's place. I felt so divided. I wanted to go with Shirl because I loved her, of course, but I wanted to stay here, too. Here in Scotland, where I felt so much at home—with Jeanie and Fiona and Torquil and, most of all, with Denny. "It's not fair," I muttered, and stared down into the moat.

"No, Carly, don't do it! Don't jump! Oh, it can't end this way!"

I turned around, and there stood Denny, clutching at his heart and grinning at me.

"Idiot," I scolded. "The moat isn't deep enough to keep goldfish happy."

Coming up behind him were Shirl and Fiona, walking arm-in-arm. "Carly," Fiona said, "you left before we could talk about our idea for you. Would you like to come back in August and stay the whole month with us?"

"Would I like . . .? Could I, Shirl?"

Shirl nodded happily. "As a reward for saving Jeanie, they would like to fly you over as their guest."

"I'm sure there are many places you'd still like to see," Fiona said.

Denny burst out laughing. "She just happens to have a list," he said.

I was too happy to say anything, so I burst out laughing, too.

*B*y the next morning, Jeanie had returned to her old routines. As she groomed Muffin, her favorite horse, she told him about her adventure. "Denny said I was brave, but Mummy says I can't tell just anyone. She wouldn't mind me telling you, though," and she gave part of her apple to the appreciative tan and white Muffin.

"Jeanie, luv—are you here, child?"

"Yes, Mummy, I'm in the stable."

She must stop saying "Mummy." If she went back to acting like a little girl, they would treat her like one, especially Nanny.

"Oh, here you are. We looked everywhere. They couldn't wait any longer. Didn't you want to say farewell?"

"Mummy, are they gone? Did Carly go without seeing me?"

"They would have missed their plane if they'd waited any longer. Pops is driving them in the van, and Dennis went along."

Jeanie took a deep breath and put on what she hoped was a mature expression. "Mum, I'd be ever so careful. May Muffin and I try to catch up with them?"

Mum laughed. "Very well. I can trust our Muffin not to run too fast. But hurry back. You and I need some time together, just the two of us."

Jeanie gave Mum a hearty kiss before jumping on the startled old horse's back. Muffin hadn't dreamed anything would be expected of him today. He'd been anticipating only the rest of Jeanie's apple.

"Come on, slowpoke Muffin," she yelled, and Muffin trotted away at a pace he felt was proper.

Happily, the van seemed only to have just left. "There they are, Muffin. On the road to Dumfries. Come on, you old dear, and I'll give you an apple all for yourself."

Perhaps Muffin understood, for he soon caught up and trotted in back of the van. "Carly," Jeanie yelled with all her might. "Carly, wait."

The van slowed, the rear window opened, and Carly thrust out her head. "Bye, Jeanie." Carly waved and waved.

"Farewell, Carly," Jeanie shouted. "Haste ye back!"

She allowed Muffin to rest, and she and Carly waved and blew kisses to each other until the van was out of sight.

Marilyn at Dundrennan Abbey, Scotland. Region: Dumfries and Galloway

About the Author

MARILYN LUDWIG IS A DEVOTED anglophile, who has journeyed throughout the UK, tip-to-tip—from Land's End to John O'Groats. She has accomplished everything on Carly's *Things I Want to Do* list.

Marilyn teaches theatre to middle grade and high school students and has written many of the plays her students have performed. She is a member of the Society of Children's Book Writers and Illustrators.

Searching for Juliette, Marilyn's YA novel, and *Miles: A Little Dog with an Eye for Friendship*, co-authored with her daughter, Kristin Ludwig (www.houseofnubs.org) were published in 2015.